"I'm not going to marry you," she blurted. "No matter what my sister tells you."

I didn't say anything at first. I was truly speechless.

"Okay," I said. "Good to know."

"Did she tell you that I was looking for a husband?"

"Not really," I said.

Another thing I had learned was not to leave someone else feeling stupid or foolish.

This seemed like one of those situations where it would be wise to put that skill to use. Besides, she seemed wary of me.

"Well," she said. "I'm not."

Dakota was quite serious.

I swept her around the ballroom, her dress outshining all the dresses the other ladies wore.

"We are going to be a good pair," I said.

"Why do you say that?" she asked, with obvious suspicion in her golden green eyes.

I smiled. She doubtless thought I missed the point.

"Because," I said. "You're not looking for a husband and I'm not looking for a wife."

I don't know why I thought that would ease her worries. I knew women better than to think that.

"I don't understand," she said. "You claimed my entire evening."

CHAMPAGNE SILVER

CHAMPAGNE SILVER

THE BECQUERELS

KATHRYN KALEIGH

To learn more about Kathryn Kaleigh, visit

www.kathrynkaleigh.com

Kathryn Kaleigh

CHAPTER 1
DAKOTA AUCLAIR

November 1868

"I do NOT need a husband."

I stood in my sister's mammoth dressing room with a hundred thousand yards of gold and white silk taffeta cascading around my waist to the floor.

I balanced on a little velvet platform with two seamstresses painstakingly measuring and pinning the hem of the dress. The taffeta rustled with each little movement.

My sister Bailey, big as a house—pregnant with her first child—sat on a blue velvet loveseat and grinned at me. She was positively glowing.

"Have a glass of champagne—for me—and enjoy yourself," she said. "You know I can't have champagne while I'm expecting."

Bailey's husband, Graham Daniels, insisted that she not touch a drop of alcohol while pregnant. To say that he was a hovering husband would be an understatement.

"These slippers are killing my feet," I said crossly. My sister insisted I wear the white leather lace-up boots for the fitting so that the length of the dress was perfect. The little one-inch heels would have been comfortable enough if they had been just a tad bit longer.

"I know," she said. "It's not my fault your foot is bigger than mine. Your boots will be ready in time for the ball tomorrow night."

The seamstresses did not complain as I shifted from one foot to the other, then steeled myself for the duration. Or a few more minutes, at least.

One of Bailey's ladies in waiting handed me a champagne flute. The bubbles always made me smile. It was, of course, the best. My sister had the best of everything. No exaggeration.

She lived in a house with eight bedrooms. Each bedroom had what she called an en suite with a bathtub and indoor plumbing.

Indoor plumbing was an unheard of luxury out here in the mountains near the little town of Whiskey Springs.

The house had a total of four stories. The entire top story was Bailey's studio for painting and sketching. Canvases stood on easels all around the room. Sometimes the paint fumes permeated the house all the way down to the first floor.

In truth, Bailey often took her canvases and paints outside or her sketchbook and charcoal pencils, but the studio was perfect for cold days and breathtaking views. Standing on the balcony outside her fourth-floor studio, in fact, we could see the town below us. And Graham swore he could see the lights of Denver from here, but I had never seen them. Bailey declined to comment.

"That dress is beautiful," Bailey said. "It makes you look like an empress."

"It seems far too extravagant for a mere masquerade ball."

"Maybe," Bailey admitted. "But isn't it fun? And since you're here to help me with the baby, the least I can do is to make sure you're happy."

"Your piano makes me plenty happy," I said, taking another sip of the smooth champagne.

We'd had a piano in Natchez, Mississippi, but when we had traveled west, we couldn't bring it. I think there were other reasons we had not brought it, but I had been too young to be included in that decision.

"Turn, just a little," one of the seamstresses said.

I turned, giving me a lovely view through one of the windows. A window in a dressing room.

The view, like all the views in the house was breathtaking. From here I could see the lawn at the back of the house.

"When did you build a gazebo?" I asked, watching as two men swept white paint on a freshly constructed gazebo.

"Oh that," Bailey said. "Graham had it built for the ball."

I started to ask why, then knew it was futile. Graham did things because he could. This gazebo looked more like a house. Flattened on the front with two French doors. It had glass windows and a steep roof.

Suitable for the climate, I mused, wondering if it had a fireplace, too, but I didn't see a chimney.

I twirled the stem of my glass and studied the clouds. It would be dark before long, but I could still see the clouds well enough. "It's going to snow," I said.

My brother, Colton, was the weather expert, but I had learned enough from him to know a few things about the weather. Besides, I had lived in the mountains for three years now. A girl learned a few things or two after that long.

Specifically, right now, I could tell by the way the clouds hovered around the mountain peaks. When they moved up, there would be fresh snow on the peaks and this time of year, that snowfall usually spread to the foothills and valleys.

There were five of us siblings. I second from the youngest. Bailey was second oldest.

Our brother was right between the four of us girls. A true middle child.

Somehow our parents had managed to have five children, one per year. Such precision.

"This is too pretty," I said. The bodice had a sweetheart neckline and long sleeves. More gold lace and layers upon layers, showing off my small waist and keeping my shoulders bare.

"Where else can I possibly wear it?"

Perhaps if I were going to a ball hosted by the Queen of England, then this would be the dress to wear. And even then, I would hope it did not outshine the queen herself.

"You can wear it anywhere," she said. "And if you happen to find a husband, then..." she shrugged and smiled mischievously.

"Please tell me you did not invite someone for me to meet." I narrowed my eyes at her.

"What makes you think I would do a thing like that?" She let her shawl drop off her shoulders and wiped her brow with a cool cloth.

Watching my sister go through these hot and cold flashes and every other miserable thing like waddling like a duck, made me think that not only did I not want a husband, but I also would think twice about having children.

"Because before you married Graham, you knew all the single men in town."

"I did not," Bailey said.

I just rolled my eyes at her. I loved my sister dearly, but she could not deny that she had a lot of beaus back in her day.

"I wouldn't do that," she said. "I would want you to have your own beau."

Not a hand-me-down. That notion was ingrained in all of

us girls.

Our mother had always made sure that all of us, even the youngest, got new dresses each season. No hand-me-downs from older sisters, unless, of course, we just wanted something.

Mother had a strong sense of fairness that she had passed along to her offspring. We'd gotten fairness and kindness from her. We'd gotten fierce survivalness from our father.

Father had been killed in the war, though, and Mother had not survived long after we got the devastating news.

I was haunted by the loss of our parents. I had been young. Fifteen. And I still have nightmares. But I never told anyone that. Not even my sisters.

"What are you going to wear?" I asked, turning the conversation away from me.

"You'll see," she said. "I think you'll like it."

I just smiled. Out of us four girls, Bailey had always been the one who kept up with fashion.

So I knew that whatever she wore, even in her huge as a house state, she would look lovely.

"All finished, Miss Bailey," the head seamstress said.

"Thank goodness," I said, gathering up the skirts to step off the platform.

"Be careful, Miss," the seamstress warned. "The hem has a thousand pins in it."

"I will be careful." I walked straight to the loveseat and plopped down next to Bailey. Then I reached down, careful to avoid the pins, and pulled off the slippers that had been killing my feet for the last hour.

"It's a beautiful dress," I said adjusting the skirts around me.

"Maybe you should take it off so it doesn't get messed up," Bailey said.

I rolled my eyes, but I knew she was right.

Even if I didn't care about masked balls, particularly, it was hard not to be excited about a dress that was fit for an empress.

CHAPTER 2
ZACHARY RIVERS

Present Time

"We can't sell," Tiffany Auclair said, standing on the fourth floor balcony of the Daniels House.

"We have to sell, Tif," Hudson Auclair said, sweeping a hand across the view. "We have the opportunity to be set for life." Hudson looked over at me. "Right? Tell her Zachary."

I didn't get the chance to say anything. It was just as well. The biting wind had me too frozen through and through to give a coherent response anyway.

"We're set right now," Tiffany insisted.

Hudson put both gloved hands on his hips. "With the money, we can move away from here. We can go to New York. We can live someplace other than here."

I could see that this was going to take awhile.

They barely noticed when I opened the door and walked inside the large open top floor. What had started out as a studio for renowned landscape and wildlife artist Bailey

Auclair, the original owner of the house, was now used for entertaining.

An outdoor grill had been installed as well as an outdoor fireplace.

Couches and chairs were scattered all around, inside and out.

I went to the gas fireplace and watched the flames licking at the faux logs. Much more efficient, but I personally would have left the fireplaces alone. There was nothing like the scent of wood burning in a fireplace on a cold night.

I hated to be part of what could easily turn into a rift between the two siblings.

My company, one of those big companies in one of those big cities that Hudson wanted to move to had sent me here for one reason and one reason only.

To acquire this house so they could turn it into a luxury hotel.

I could honestly understand both arguments. I could see Hudson's point. He wanted to take the millions and run. He was more of a male fashionista, not an outdoorsy type person. He didn't realize—or maybe he didn't care—that his money wouldn't last long in New York, but it wasn't my place to tell him.

I could see his sister's point, too. She was still young. She could still have a family. Still live here and enjoy this house that had been handed down through the generations that came before her. And Tiffany was an outdoorsy person. Still living in the house and working from home, she hiked almost every day.

And there was a third viewpoint. One that I had to concern myself with. As a hotel, thousands of people could enjoy this place every year. It could be a grand hotel, rivaling even THE Grand Hotel on Mackinac Island. Well, maybe not exactly, but in a different way. A much smaller scale.

I had to keep my eyes on that one. That was my job.

The door opened and the two siblings came inside. Tiffany went straight to the fireplace, holding her hands out to the warm flames.

"We decided to wait," Hudson said, going straight to the minibar and pouring himself a glass of wine. "We'll wait until after the fundraiser tomorrow before we decide. To give us time to sleep on it."

"Good choice," I said, although I saw it for what it was. It was stalling.

I could already predict the outcome.

They would sell. They would sell because Hudson was blinded by the dollar signs. And since he had moved away to Denver long ago, he didn't have the sentimentality for the area that Tiffany did.

I also knew that he would regret it one day. And if he didn't regret selling, he would regret strong arming his sister into it.

This place meant something to her. She had every right to keep it.

"If you'll excuse me," I said. "I have to go into town to pick up my tux."

I didn't tell them that I had three in my closet at my home in New York, but I hadn't foreseen the need to bring formal clothing to a house in the middle of the mountains.

Unfortunately, that put me over more in Hudson's camp. And I hated that.

I hated it because I agreed with Tiffany on just how beautiful and special this place was.

Thank God it ultimately wasn't my decision to make.

I honestly knew I would struggle with the decision. For me I would have to weigh in whether or not I would have heirs.

Tiffany and Hudson had no heirs. But they still had time.

In the meantime, I would be attending the fundraiser they were holding here tomorrow night. The fundraiser had nothing to do with the sale of the place, at least not directly. Indirectly, it had everything to do with it.

Tiffany had opened up the house to an art gallery in town raising money for a charity. Since this had been Bailey Auclair's home, it seemed appropriate to hold the fundraiser here. What I knew was that they were awarding Tiffany a fee for the venue.

The house was expensive to maintain and needed some work. That's where I came in.

The event was significant in that it might be the first of many such fundraisers to be held in what was currently known as the Daniels House. What was to become a destination called the Daniels House Hotel outside of the little town of Whiskey Springs.

I walked down to my room on the second floor.

Bailey Auclair must have set some kind of record on the number of paintings she had done. There was one on every wall. It was my understanding that they had been thinned out over the years. At one point the house was all but papered with them and she had painted a mural on in each of the five third floor bedrooms. The bedroom that had belonged to her five children.

Only one of those murals still existed. It was a lovely mountain scene with wildlife including a flying eagle, an elk, and chipmunks.

It would have been a travesty if they had painted over it.

It was a shame they had painted over any of them. They would be perfect for the hotel rooms.

It was a great loss.

But what was left could be protected.

If I did my job well enough.

CHAPTER 3
DAKOTA

*T*he cold early afternoon air kept the guests pressed inside.

I had been right. It was snowing. Beautiful, soft snowflakes. Not a blizzard. So hopefully all the guests would be able to go home in the morning if not tonight.

Bailey and Graham had set up pallets on the second floor of the house for overnight guests.

But for now, guests were still spilling in. People wanted to see the house. I knew most people came for that, if nothing else.

I would not deny that the house was something to see. It was aglow with candle light. And the air was scented with fresh flowers everywhere. Daffodils. Poinsettias. Daisies.

A small four-man orchestra played in the ball room, providing what was supposed to be a joyful background.

I stood in the foyer next to my sister and Graham. There was a lull in the incoming guests, but another carriage was making its way up toward the front circle drive.

"I should go," I said to Bailey. "I don't have to meet everyone."

She put a hand on my arm. "Stay," she said. "I like having you here."

One of the guests came up to speak with Graham and the two men stepped away.

"See," she said. "You're keeping me from standing by myself."

"Very well," I said.

"Are your boots hurting your feet?" she asked.

"My boots are fine. I hardly notice them."

"What is it, then?"

"These people are all strangers to me," I said. "There were so many people, I could not remember their names if I'd had to.

"I don't know a lot of them either," Bailey said with a worried glance over her shoulder. "And I'm sure all of them were invited."

She looked back at me and smiled. "But we'll dance and enjoy the evening, right?"

"Of course," I said. But I knew our younger sister Elise would have been better at this. But Elise was at away at school. I was the only available sister to keep Bailey company.

"At least let me get you some punch," I said.

"Very well," she said. "As long as you get some for yourself as well."

I turned and took a step.

"And where's your dance card?" she asked.

I reached into my pocket and pulled out the little dance card I had hoped to keep hidden away. Held it up for her to see.

"Put it on," she said as I walked away.

So with that, I escaped the duty of greeting guests, at least for the moment.

My dress rustled as I navigated my way through the guests toward the refreshment table. My dress was by far the prettiest and more elegant than anyone else's.

Even my sister wore a sedate gown in a deep solid

burgundy. A high neckline and long sleeve befitting a lady in her condition.

It made me wonder all the more what she was up to by outfitting me in such a lavish gown.

I had my suspicions to be sure, but so far, I'd seen no eligible bachelors that she might be thinking to introduce me to.

I had no interest in being courted by anyone right now. I had my winter planned out. Keep my sister company until the baby came. Then help her with the newborn. She had a full library of books that I looked forward to losing myself in.

It was going to be a long winter, snowed in up here on the mountain. But I didn't mind. I rather looked forward to it.

As long as we were snowed in, we had no social obligations. And that suited me just perfectly.

As I reached the refreshment area, one of Bailey's ladies in waiting handing me a glass of punch.

"I need one for my sister, too," I said.

"Nonsense," the woman, Anna, said. "I'll take it to her. You just enjoy yourself."

Before I could protest, Anna had already taken off on her singular purpose. Bailey hated when I called her personal maids ladies in waiting, but I found it quite descriptive.

It wasn't their fault. Bailey had a way that drew people to her. Not just men, but women as well. Men wanted to be around her and ladies wanted to be her.

I took the opportunity to walk down the wide hallway leading to the back of the house.

Although I had not lied about the boots not hurting my feet, I was quite tired from just standing for so long. Surely one of the ladies in waiting would bring her a chair.

Refusing to make it my problem, I sat on one of the little velvet benches.

It couldn't hurt to just take a break from everyone.

CHAPTER 4
ZACHARY

*T*he Association of Whiskey Springs Arts—AWSA—knew how to put on a party.

Black tie waiters, all perfectly groomed carrying trays of champagne and hors d'oeuvres.

A small orchestra playing soothing, unobtrusive music.

Elegantly dressed men and women, who obviously had generous pocketbooks, milled about.

It was nice to see that Tiffany Auclair had donated one of her great-great-great... great grandmother's paintings. I hadn't taken the time to do the family tree. Even though she had only donated one for sale, there were others on the walls to admire.

Bailey Auclair had been an excellent, creative artist and she was prolific as the day was long. Her body of work was quite impressive. Each painting, each sketch was named and even though the dates were on some of them, I was quickly learning to tell her earlier work from her later work. Some of her earlier work was surprisingly better than what she did later.

I saw a lot of variety.

And she had not been afraid to try new things. She'd even done some portraits of her family.

With a glass of champagne in one hand, I took some time to explore a cozy little sitting area with at least two dozen framed charcoal sketches of what looked to be her family members.

"There you are," Hudson, said, looking a bit flustered. "I've been looking all over for you."

"I'm right here," I said. "Is there something you need to discuss?"

"Yes." Hudson looked over his shoulder. "But…" He grabbed me by the arm and guided me away from the sitting area toward the hallway.

"We need someplace quiet," he said. "Private."

He wasn't going to find a private area inside the house. Everywhere we turned there were other people wandering about. Even as we left the portrait sitting area, a couple of people wandered in.

My guess was that many of the people had come just to see the house.

The house had mostly been private, at least for the last hundred years or so. That meant that no one outside of family and a few chosen guests had seen the inside.

That was the part that helped me justify my job of trying to convince the Auclairs to sell. My company was big enough that they could renovate the house in such a way that would attract guests from all over the world. And in addition to the renovations, they had the marketing capabilities to make it happen.

If you were going to do something, you had to market it. Otherwise people would not know it was there.

I suspected that within two years, the eight bedrooms could be booked years in advance. I'd seen it happen. There was an old hotel in New York that had started out as a gangster house.

Now it was virtually impossible to get a room there. I had procured that deal. It had been much like this one. Family divided. That one was easier though because the owners—both female—were older, no children, and were past their child-bearing years.

I followed Hudson down the hallway and outside to the veranda.

The cold wind sliced right through my jacket.

There were people out here as well, most of them dressed more appropriately for the weather than we were.

"This is not a good—"

"Come," Hudson said. "Let's go to the gazebo. It's heated."

I followed him down a little stone path to the gazebo. The gazebo looked more like a house. Glass walls on all sides and double French doors. Necessary if it was going to be used any time other than the warmest of summer days.

I was curious what it had been used for over the years.

As we neared, I saw that there was an endless swimming pool behind it. From here, it looked like the end of the pool fell off the side of the mountain.

"Who built the pool?" I asked as we stepped inside the gazebo. And where did they get the money?

"I think Tiffany built it herself," Hudson said, waving it off. "The heat's not on."

The heat was definitely not on.

"Wait here," Hudson said. "I'll go outside and flip the switch."

"Good idea," I said. An even better idea would be to go back inside into the warmth of the house. Tiffany obviously did not want anyone in here or she would have turned on the heat and made it inviting.

Not only was it cold, it needed attention. It needed sweeping, for one. Leaves had blown inside and left to decay.

Puzzled, I sat down on one of the benches and closed my eyes.

Think about warm places.

I imagined my parents sitting on a beach in Florida

drinking Pina coladas. Nice place to vacation now and then, but I wouldn't want to live there. They, however, were enjoying their early retirement. Had a nice condo in a retirement community. They were content.

As their only child, I should probably visit them more often. Yet I somehow managed to convince myself that they were content without me impinging on their lives.

Funny how people could justify just about anything with no more than a little effort.

I glanced at my watch.

Hudson should have been back. He was just going to step out and turn on the heat.

I waited about another minute. My teeth were chattering.

This was just about all I could handle. If this cost me the deal, then so be it.

If I continued to sit here, they would find me out here, frozen.

In a gazebo that was supposed to be heated.

I opened the door.

How long had I been out here?

Snowflakes were falling. Feathery soft. Big. Drifty.

My cell phone hadn't been working well up here, so I had not been keeping up with the weather. Still this was quite unexpected.

I didn't mind the snow. At least not when there were snow plows. Up here... I wasn't so sure.

I gave a cursory look around for Hudson. He must have gone back inside without me.

Having enough with this already, I dashed off toward the house. Reaching the covered veranda, I brushed off the snowflakes and stomped my feet.

The orchestra had changed up its tune a bit. It sounded even more classical.

Stepping inside, I headed straight for the fireplace in the

small parlor at the back of the house. It was a little less crowded here.

I stood there for probably five minutes before I realized that not only were the flames real, the wood was real, too.

I hadn't realized that there were any wood burning fireplaces left in the house.

Perplexed, I turned around.

The fundraising event had changed a bit since I had gone outside and come back in.

A waiter stopped. Took one look at me.

He reached into his pocket and pulled out an embroidered black mask.

"Sir," he said, a quick glance over his shoulder before he handed it to me. "Put your mask on. Mistress is a stickler for it."

I took the mask from him and he walked off.

The guests had all morphed into wearing ball gowns and frock coats.

And all of them had masks over their eyes.

CHAPTER 5
DAKOTA

"Miss Dakota," Anna, the head lady in waiting, said. "Mistress Bailey sent me to look for you. She sent me to plead with you to not make her come look for you. She's exhausted. And I honestly don't think she can take another step without toppling over."

Toying with the dance card at my wrist, I followed Anna toward the back parlor.

"It's time to put on your mask, Miss," she said and handed me the gold, glittering mask that matched my dress. I had made it myself. Making the masks had been one of Bailey's projects.

I stood still while Anna situated the mask over my eyes then tied it in a bow at the back of my head.

I could be whoever I wanted to be now. I didn't have to be Dakota Auclair, Bailey Auclair's little sister. I could be Empress Dakota Auclair from a foreign country. Here to visit her relatives in the country.

Smiling at the ludicrous idea, I stepped into the parlor and saw Bailey talking with a masked man I hadn't seen before.

Even with the mask, I knew I hadn't seen him before. I knew because he was wearing strange clothes.

He looked up. Saw me.

I stopped abruptly, my skirts swaying over the hoops.

So this was the man my sister had invited for me to meet. The man she intended to introduce me to in hopes that we would like each other enough to be married.

Like my fictional self, he must be from a foreign country. I'd never seen a man dressed like him. His black pants and coat were obviously of highest quality, but the style... oh my... I felt sorry for Graham. If this was the new style, then Bailey would soon have Graham dressed in this fashion.

My sister liked to keep up with the latest styles. This man's coat was much too fitted and even more too short. And he wasn't wearing a hat. I gave him the benefit of the doubt on that one. Perhaps he had lost it in the snow on his way here. Or perhaps one of the ladies in waiting had taken it someplace to dry.

I turned around on my heels and started walking back in the direction I had come.

"Dakota," my sister called out. I stopped. Took a deep breath and lifted my chin.

I would simply meet the fellow. Get it over with, then go about my business.

My sister was determined that I have someone on my dance card tonight. It might as well be this hapless fellow.

My voluminous skirts flowing around me, I turned and walked back to Bailey and the mysterious guest.

"Hello," I said, looking at Bailey with narrowed eyes, then forced a smile onto my lips as I looked at the stranger.

But I didn't say anything to him. Instead, I found myself speechless as I gazed into his piercing blue eyes.

He was nothing like I expected after a simple first glance at his attire.

"This is Zachary Rivers," she said. "This is my sister Dakota."

"It's nice to meet you," he said. "Both of you."

"My sister's dance card has some space on it, I believe," Bailey said.

I cut my eyes at her.

"Zachary is in town on business," she said.

"My sister seems to think we should dance," I said, holding up my dance card in his general direction.

"Then we don't want to disappoint her, do we?" He held my dance card, seemed to study it, choosing his dance carefully.

Then he signed his name and smiled at me again. "I'll see you shortly then," he said.

So he had chosen one of the first dances.

I walked to the fireplace and held my hands to the flames.

Zachary didn't seem all that bad, other than his strange clothes.

I suppose we were alike in that way. He might find it strange that I wore a dress fit for an empress to a simple masked ball in the country.

He had only signed my dance card once, so he wasn't a presumptuous man. That was a good quality to have, I suppose.

With my back to him, I lifted my dance card to see his signature.

He had signed it only once, but he had boldly signed his name diagonally across all the lines.

Mon Dieu.

He had claimed ALL my dances.

CHAPTER 6
ZACHARY

*S*ince I didn't see Tiffany or Hudson anywhere, I thought it best to stay to myself until Hudson showed back up. He had seemed rather uncharacteristically flustered.

Most of all, I wanted this to be a smooth transaction and I definitely wanted to get out of here before I was trapped in a snow storm.

I didn't even know if they had snow plows in this area. If they didn't, we were going to have problems.

No one seemed to be concerned though and I found that oddly comforting.

The music was smooth. Professional. People milled about, talking. Laughing. Champagne and punch flowed freely.

It was an idyllic scene.

Unfortunately, it hadn't lasted more than a few minutes before I was approached by a young lady very much pregnant.

She introduced herself as Mrs. Daniels.

Pregnant Mrs. Daniles wanted me to dance with her sister. And from what I had seen, that didn't seem like it would be much of a hardship.

The girl in the golden dress caught my attention the moment I saw her approaching.

All the ladies here tonight were wearing ball gowns, but hers stood out as the most elegantly stunning. The long full-skirted ball gown shimmered in the candlelight.

It was a preposterous idea, but everyone appeared to have changed clothes while I was out in the gazebo with Hudson.

They appeared to have changed into nineteenth century garb as easily as they had put on their masks.

The music of a waltz began and people started making their way to the ballroom. The buzz of excited conversation increased.

I excused myself from Mrs. Daniles and went in search of the girl named Dakota in the golden dress. Standing out like a sparkling gem, she wasn't hard to find.

"I think this is our cue," I said holding out a hand.

She looked at my hand with a little scowl between her delicate brows, then tucked one of her gloved hands in the crook of my elbow.

"You're not from here," she said as we walked side by side down the wide hallway. Several other couples walked ahead and behind us.

"What gave it away?" I asked.

"Your attire is… different."

"I see that," I said. "This is all I had with me."

She looked at me sideways. "I understand. You should know. My sister finds fashion very important."

"Speaking of your sister, it looks like you're going to be an aunt soon," he said as we stepped into the ballroom. The ambiance was stunning. The room, like the rest of the house now, was lit by even more candlelight. Chandeliers with a thousand wide and tall candles.

I pulled Dakota into a waltz that matched what everyone else was doing.

I was good at blending in. Blending in was an ability that had helped me close countless deals. It was a well-researched fact that people trusted people who are similar to them.

So I had learned how to make myself seem similar to others.

Tonight I was a man who enjoyed art and views from the fourth floor balcony on a snowy night in the mountains.

As we swirled around the ballroom, Dakota looked up at me. There was something enchanting about her sparkling green eyes. A rare color. As I looked closely, I saw that little shards of gold seemed to reflect off her dress.

I was reminded of the mariners who were lured to their death because they had been unable to resist the lure of the sirens.

Dakota was a siren, I decided.

"I'm not going to marry you," she blurted. "No matter what my sister tells you."

I didn't say anything at first. I was truly speechless.

"Okay," I said. "Good to know."

"Did she tell you that I was looking for a husband?"

"Not really," I said.

Another thing I had learned was not to leave someone else feeling stupid or foolish.

This seemed like one of those situations where it would be wise to put that skill to use. Besides, she seemed wary of me.

"Well," she said. "I'm not."

Dakota was quite serious.

I swept her around the ballroom, her dress outshining all the dresses the other ladies wore.

"We are going to be a good pair," I said.

"Why do you say that?" she asked, with obvious suspicion in her golden green eyes.

I smiled. She doubtless thought I missed the point.

"Because," I said. "You're not looking for a husband and I'm not looking for a wife."

I don't know why I thought that would ease her worries. I knew women better than to think that.

"I don't understand," she said. "You claimed my entire evening."

I grinned guiltily. "You're right. I probably shouldn't have done that. But I have to admit that I wanted to be the guy dancing with the girl in the most beautiful dress at the party."

She looked at me a moment, her gaze intent.

"You speak with a silver tongue," she said. "You can't be trusted."

I laughed. "You speak with a blunt tongue."

She smiled a little and lowered her gaze. I imagined it was something she was rarely called out on.

This girl was fascinating. I could not remember the last time I had had such a stimulating conversation about absolutely nothing that made sense.

And my plan backfired. I was the one who relaxed.

This promised to be a fascinating night after all.

CHAPTER 7
DAKOTA

*S*weeping around the ballroom in my golden dress, I really did feel like an empress.

It didn't matter that I was with a man who wore funny looking clothes. He was actually an exceptionally skilled dancer. Even more, he had a gentle touch about him. I could tell by the way he gently held my hand. By the way his hand rested lightly on my waist.

I liked the way other people looked at us with admiration and perhaps envy as we swept past them on the dance floor.

Perhaps it wasn't such a bad way to spend an evening. No one knew me and no one knew him.

We did not even know each other.

"You're from here," he said.

"Whiskey Springs," I said. "I'm staying with my sister to help with the baby."

"That's admirable of you."

"Family," I said with a shrug.

"I don't have any brothers or sisters," he said.

"Oh. I'm sorry."

"It's okay," he said. "I don't miss what I don't know."

"Maybe," I said. I don't think I agreed with that statement, but I gave him a pass on it since he was doing a decent job of making small talk with someone he had never met before.

"Do you know these people?" he asked.

"Not a single one other than my sister and her husband."

We waltzed past the refreshment table. A formally dressed server waited to pick up a tray filled with champagne. Another waited for a tray filled with punch glasses. My family had been well-enough off, comfortable really, but this was by far a step over the top.

"But I'm not originally from here," I said.

"Let me guess," he said. "I'm good at this."

I smiled. Waited.

"South Carolina."

I laughed. "You're not so good as you think. You're in the right quadrant though."

"Well, you're definitely a southern girl," he said.

I batted my lashes at him in my best Bailey imitation. "Natchez, Mississippi. Born and bred."

He laughed.

"Where are you from?" I asked after he swept me around in a circle.

"Want to venture a guess?"

"Somewhere up north," I said, feeling a little out of breath. Whether from the dancing or the way he looked at me with those icy blue eyes, I couldn't say.

"New York City by way of Indiana."

"Did you fight in the war?" I asked, not sure I really wanted to know. My father had been killed by Yankees. It was something I preferred not to think about.

"The war?" He seemed a bit perplexed by the question. "I've never been in the military."

"That's good," I said. At least I didn't have to worry about dancing with the enemy who may or may not have been the man who killed my father.

"Would you like to take a break?" he asked. "Take a look at some of the paintings."

"I wouldn't mind a break," I said. I'd seen all the paintings, but I liked the idea of seeing them with him.

He took my hand and led me toward the long, wide hallway.

He plucked two glasses of champagne from a server's tray and handed one to me.

Considerate. I mentally added that to his list of good traits.

So far I hadn't seen anything I didn't like, excluding, of course, the way he was dressed and I had to admit that I was getting used to that.

His suit may have been different from everyone else's, but he was quite handsome and striking in it. I think he would have been handsome in whatever he wore.

Then again, most everyone looked good behind their masks. The masks were an equalizing device for most.

As we walked, Zachary seemed to be looking for someone. If he hadn't been holding my hand, I would have thought he was looking for another lady.

It worried me a bit that I didn't like that idea.

I reminded myself that I was merely taking a page from Bailey's playbook and enjoying the man's company for the evening.

CHAPTER 8
ZACHARY

I held on to Dakota's hand as we walked along the west hallway. There were a lot of people here and, even though she would be easy enough to find, I didn't want to lose sight of her.

Someone had moved the paintings. They had been lined up here in this hallway earlier.

"What do you think they did with the paintings?" I asked, mostly to myself, since I did not expect her to know any more than I did.

"What paintings?" she asked.

"The ones on display," I said. "The ones for sale."

"I didn't know any of them were for sale." She was cute when her brows gathered in confusion.

"Anything can be bought for the right price," I said.

I didn't care for the look she was giving me now. The confusion had changed into suspicion.

"You don't agree," I said, slightly amused. That told me Dakota was still young and idealistic. Not bad traits to have. Sometimes I wouldn't mind being a bit less jaded myself.

But in my work, I saw how money made people do things

they normally wouldn't. Like sell a piece of property that had been in their family for generations.

I felt rather fortunate that my life was simple. My parents had not accumulated anything to pass along to me. I guess someday I'd have to dispose of a condo in Florida, but nothing otherwise. I found it freeing.

And that helped me do what I did. Since I viewed owning things I wasn't using as clutter, I could genuinely, without guilt, convey that viewpoint to others.

I had an enviable track record. One that had made me sought after in my field.

One thing, probably negative, about what I did was that I had not taken the time it took to cultivate a long-term romantic relationship. I'd had a couple of girlfriends, but it hadn't taken long for them to give up on me and move on. They had complained about all the travel I did for work. It was funny, because that was the very thing that had attracted them in first place.

"Do you really want to see some paintings?" she asked.

"I wouldn't mind." This was an art gallery related fundraiser, after all. It seemed like the thing to do.

Dakota didn't seem to understand the purpose of a fundraiser. To sell things to raise money.

She led me around to another room off the hallway, grabbed a candle from a sconce on the wall, and opened the door.

"This is a reading room," she said, lowering her voice even though no one else was near enough to hear.

The room had three oversized settees in the middle with lamps next to each one. Lamps with no lightbulb. Just a candle holder.

She set the candle in the holder of one of the lamps.

I took a minute to study the design. Ingenuous. I had never seen anything like it before.

The wall opposite the door was all windows, including French doors, much like the gazebo. It was dark outside now and snowing harder. In fact, little piles of snow were accumulating on the windowsills.

Two of the walls had floor to ceiling bookcases packed with books of all kinds. Leather and paperback. There was a ladder attached to each one of them.

"Back here," Dakota said.

I turned around to see a whole wall covered in paintings.

I needed light.

"Can I bring this?" I asked, bringing the candle lamp after she nodded.

She proceeded to give me a tour.

"The ones on the left are from when Bailey lived in Whiskey Springs. The ones on the right were done after she moved here."

They were all landscapes. Rugged mountain peaks. Rushing rivers. Quaking aspens.

"All originals," I said. All signed by Bailey Auclair.

Lakes. Sunsets. Thunderstorms.

"If the name of the painting isn't on the front," Dakota said. "It's on the back."

"All named," I said.

"I don't know how she keeps up with them all," Dakota said, absently wandering toward one of the bookcases.

"Must be a system of some sort," I said. "Otherwise she would have repeated herself."

"I don't think so," she said, sliding a book from one of the packed bookshelves.

I was no art expert, but I had been around it enough to know when to be impressed. And I was impressed by Bailey Aucliar.

"She has one called Lavender Blue Number Two," Dakota said over her shoulder. "Actually..." She turned and pointed to a painting on the right. "That's Lavender Blue, the first one. Not sure what she did with the second one."

"You know a lot about her work," I said.

"I'm around it enough. I should know a lot about it." She opened the book in her hands and stepped close to the candle to read.

The more I was around Dakota, the more mysterious she became.

"Are you friends with Tiffany?" I asked.

"Who's Tiffany?" She glanced at me, then went back to her book.

She would have made so much more sense if she had simply been friends with Tiffany. Or even Hudson. I didn't ask about Hudson. If she didn't know about Tiffany, she wouldn't know Hudson.

Yet… she seemed to be an expert on Bailey Auclair.

She was a mystery I intended to figure out.

And besides that, she was stunningly beautiful. Naturally beautiful. She wasn't wearing a stitch of makeup.

"What?" she asked, catching me looking at her.

"Nothing," I said. But I meant everything.

I wanted to know everything about her.

CHAPTER 9
DAKOTA

I wasn't sure why I had brought Zachary to my favorite room in the house.

He wanted to see paintings so I had brought him here.

If he really wanted to see Bailey's paintings, I could have taken him up to her studio, but that was private. Something Bailey would have to do.

He seemed fascinated by them.

Pretending to read, I studied him from beneath my lashes.

It was almost like he knew her work. As far as I knew, my sister hadn't sold any of her work. But she didn't tell me everything.

"Do you own one of her paintings?" I asked, closing the book.

"No," I said. "But a lot of people do."

I slid the book back on the bookcase. I would come back later and take my time choosing something to read. After I got started with an author, I usually read everything I could find by them.

Maybe he was confusing Bailey with someone else.

How many Bailey Auclairs could there be?

"How do you know her?"

"By reputation," he said without hesitation.

"I didn't know she had one." I moved to stand next to him. Or as close as I could in this dress with miles and miles of silk taffeta belling out between us.

He looked at me with a perplexed expression. I just shrugged.

"You know her work," he said. "And yet…" He was looking at me with an intensity that made my heart beat too fast. In a way that made me think about walking into his arms.

This feeling was foreign to me. I had been young, just at the age when boys would have started to come courting, when the war started. All those boys had gone to war. And they hadn't come back.

If they had, I didn't know. My family had gone west. And we had gone into survival mode.

That had changed now that my two older sisters were married. I never saw Andrea, the oldest any more. She lived in Denver. It was only a few hours ride from here on horseback, but the terrain was difficult.

Andrea's husband, Reed, couldn't visit Whiskey Springs.

No one talked about why. But I knew why. I was the one who had been there. The one who had turned around just as Reed's hand slipped from Andrea's. I had been the first one to my sister's side.

I knew that Reed had been from a different time. From the future. If Reed ever went back to Whiskey Springs and walked through the door to our house again, he might go back to the future and never come back. So he stayed away.

That was something my siblings and I never talked about amongst each other and we certainly couldn't talk about it with anyone else. We would be carted off to the insane asylum.

Zachary reminded me a bit of Reed. I couldn't say why,

really. Maybe it was the way he walked. Or the way he talked. It was something I would have to think about. Later.

I turned away from him, walking to the window to look out into the darkness. I pressed my nose against the cold glass and saw the snow falling down in the moonlight.

It was breathtakingly beautiful and it was deadly.

"If it doesn't stop snowing, you all could be stranded here," I said.

He was silent a minute. I looked over my shoulder, thinking maybe he had left.

For some reason, that scared me. Again, reminded me of Reed.

I shook my head. That was irrational.

But, I looked over my shoulder anyway.

He left the candle lamp there and reached my side in an instant.

He put a hand on my elbow and looked down at me. He was a full head taller than I was. Somehow I hadn't noticed it so much when we had been dancing. But now, with him standing here, his hand on my elbow, he made me feel small. Delicate. Protected.

I looked up into his eyes.

"That would be bad, wouldn't it?" he asked.

"What's that?"

He smiled. "To have us all stranded here."

I swallowed hard. My breath was coming in shallow.

"No," I whispered, shaking my head.

Zachary put a hand gently on my chin and lowered his head toward mine. My eyes fluttered closed and my lips parted.

He pressed his lips gently to mine.

The orchestra music faded into the background. Everything else ceased to exist.

This. This kiss was everything.

CHAPTER 10
ZACHARY

I had known I was going to kiss Dakota from the moment I first saw her.

But with her standing there in front of the window, the snow falling silently in the moonlight behind her, I knew I had to seize the moment.

She said *you all* could be stranded. Not *we* will be stranded.

I didn't understand her. She was different and mysterious. And lovely.

Even as I kissed her, I knew this would not work. I lived in New York. She lived in Whiskey Springs.

As I savored the feel of her lips against mine, I had a flash of inspiration. I could take her with me to New York. Maybe she could travel with me. If she had the time to take care of her sister, then maybe she had a job with flexibility. A photographer maybe. A writer. A consultant.

I needed to know more about her.

Sweeping a hand over her cheek, I gazed at her. Her face was flushed, her eyes still closed.

"Dakota," I said. Her eyes opened. Bedroom eyes.

She licked her lips. I was lost. Right here and now.

Just like that.

I took a deep breath. Went with it.

"What do you do?" I asked.

She blinked. In confusion. "What do you mean?"

"For—"

Something crashed outside. Wood splintering. Glass breaking.

The crash was followed by silence. The orchestra stopped. Not smoothly, but discordantly. So they had heard it also.

I suddenly remembered that I hadn't seen Hudson since I'd been in the gazebo. It had been snowing so I hadn't really looked for him anywhere else.

He could still be out there.

"I need to see what the commotion is about," I said, reluctantly releasing my hold on her.

"Wait here," I said.

Ignoring me, she followed as I hurried down the wide hallway lit only by candlelight.

I didn't blame her. I would not have waited either.

People gathered at the windows, peering out toward the gazebo.

Someone opened the door and stepped outside into the snow.

Feeling somewhat responsible for Hudson, even though I knew I wasn't, I went out, too.

The snow was heavier than I expected. Heavier than it had been earlier.

It didn't take long to discover that a tree had fallen in front of the gazebo. I couldn't tell if it had actually fallen on top of the gazebo or not, but it certainly had sounded like it.

I wasn't able to shake the feeling that Hudson was out here. Injured. And I had abandoned him.

But since it had led to me meeting Dakota, I refused to feel guilty about that.

But I had to do what I could to help him.

Other men were just standing there, looking around at the tree.

They didn't know that there was a man injured out there. And the more I thought about it, the more I was convinced that Hudson was out here. Hurt.

Pushing my way through branches, tearing my shirt and breaking branches, I made it to the gazebo doors.

"Hudson," I called.

One of the doors was smashed, maybe both. The door fell off its hinges as I pulled on it. Shoving it aside, broken glass crunching under my feet, I stepped inside the gazebo.

It was warm inside. Hudson had managed to turn on the heat.

But there was no sign of Hudson.

I needed to get back out. To check behind the gazebo. Underneath the tree.

Turning around, I faced the French doors.

The glass was not shattered, the doors were not busted.

The doors were intact.

My ears buzzed as I carefully touched one of the doorknobs, turned it, and pushed it open.

There was no tree down.

It was still cold, but…

No snow.

CHAPTER 11
DAKOTA

I stepped outside onto the veranda into the cold and watched men standing around, scratching their heads at the tree that had fallen onto the gazebo. The brand-new gazebo that had just been finished this morning.

Oddly enough, there was a full moon tonight and clouds shifted just so, giving us a good view of the aspen tree lying in front, maybe onto, the gazebo. It was hard to tell from here.

Zachary was the only person who didn't just stand around.

He ran headlong, crashing through the branches. He called somebody's name. Hudson?

Then he was quiet.

All was quiet out here. Inside the house, people talked. And gaped. Speculated.

The storm must have knocked the tree down.

Did you see that man run up in there? Do you know him?

It fell right on top of the gazebo.

I didn't think so. I could see the top of the gazebo from where I was standing.

The cold barely registered with me.

I paced from one end of the veranda to the other. And back.

Zachary did not come out.

I could still feel his lips on mine. Even in the cold, I could feel that kiss.

I gathered up my skirts and darted down the steps. Hurried across the lawn, my boots getting covered in freshly fallen snow.

"Somebody help him," I said, looking at the two men standing on my left.

Nobody moved.

I looked to my right. There was an older fellow standing there. He looked vaguely familiar. "Help him," I said.

The older fellow went to the tree, but the limbs were too much for him to push through.

"Never mind," I said. "I'll do it."

"Miss. Wait."

Enough with waiting. Zachary was in there and something had happened. He was still in there.

I broke off one of the limbs that blocked my path and ducked beneath the next one.

Soon I worked my way to the gazebo doors.

My boots crunched over broken glass as I stepped through the doors one hanging by one hinge. Into the dark gazebo. I realized too late that I couldn't see a thing in here.

"Zachary?" I called out. Holding out my hands, I moved blindly around the gazebo.

Found nothing.

By then, enough men had rallied to start removing the tree.

I heard Graham, Bailey's husband yelling at them. "Get that tree out of there." Then I heard someone calling my own name.

As they pulled the tree away, I could see now. I could see well enough to know that Zachary was not here.

I dropped onto the floor and lowered my head.

Zachary had pushed his way into this gazebo and vanished.

Just like Reed.

And I knew.

Everything made sense now.

His odd clothing.

How he knew Bailey Auclair by reputation.

Zachary was from the future.

CHAPTER 12
ZACHARY

I had always been psychologically sound. I'd never had any anxiety or depression. I was well-rounded. Extraverted.

First in my graduating class. Most likely to succeed.

MBA in marketing. Columbia University.

A regular guy. A regular successful guy.

But right now, I would consider myself anything other than psychologically sound.

I stood in the door of the gazebo. The warm air from the heater at my back. Cold wind hitting me in the face.

It was not snowing. At least not yet. And had not been snowing.

The windows of the house reflected warm morning sun.

It was morning.

And the house was quiet. No music. I saw no guests.

And even more noticeable. There was no fallen tree.

I backed up and sat down in one of the two chairs inside the gazebo.

My thoughts had scattered into a thousand different directions.

I'd had a few sips of champagne, no more.

I had scrambled through the limbs of a fallen tree to get in here.

I lowered my head into my hands, pressing my fingers against my brow.

Maybe something had happened to me. Maybe I had passed out.

Dakota.

I got up and started across the lawn.

I had to find Dakota.

"Zachary?" Hudson called, coming out the back door of the house.

I stopped.

"Where have you been?" he asked, his eyes flicking over me from head to toe. "We looked everywhere for you."

"I was waiting for you," I said. "In the gazebo."

"What? Get in here. Get warm."

I followed him inside, but I couldn't make sense of it.

Stepping into the house, through the back door, I was struck with how different everything looked.

Gone were the candles. In their place were bright overhead lights.

"I'll be right back," I said, taking off down the hallway without him.

I went straight back into the library where I had been standing when I heard the tree fall. Where I had kissed Dakota.

First of all, Dakota wasn't there. Second, there a large oversized desk in the center of the room. And third, there was only one painting on the wall.

I immediately recognized it.

Lavender Blue.

Hudson stood at the door. Watching me warily.

"There was a girl," I said. "In a gold ball gown. Dakota."

Hudson was looking at me like I had fallen off my rocker.

He shook his head. "Where have you been?" he asked again.

"I've been… here," I said.

"Zachary," he said. "You were gone for two days."

I held onto the back of the nearest armchair for support.

"No," I shook my head.

"Hudson," he said. "You're bleeding."

I looked down at my arms. My sleeves were torn and he was right. My arms were scratched and bleeding.

Hudson reached in his pocket. Pulled out a cell phone—my cell phone—and handed it to me. "It's been ringing off the hook," he said. "I didn't answer it."

I had some missed calls. A few voicemails. A ton of text messages.

I'd deal with that later. Since I didn't see anybody on there by the name of Dakota, it didn't hold much interest to me.

But according to my cell phone, he was right. I had been gone for two days.

What the— I straightened. Put one hand on my waist and took a minute to steady myself.

"Where was I?"

"You tell me," Hudson said. He walked to the window. Looked out. "I turned on the heat in the gazebo and came back. You were gone."

"How did you get this?" I held up my cell phone.

Hudson turned. Looked at me. "You left it in the gazebo."

"Can I get a drink?" I asked.

"Good idea."

I sat down. Let Hudson get me a drink. I didn't even care what. Just something to help me settle. Something real to hold in my hand.

Hudson came back, handed me a scotch. "Why are you wearing a mask over your eyes?" he asked.

CHAPTER 13
DAKOTA

I stood perfectly still in the middle of the guest room that was my room as long as I wanted it to be.

One of Bailey's ladies in waiting, Anna, a kind young lady, probably thirty or so, with a nice smile, helped me get out of the lovely golden dress. Ruined beyond repair. I had lost my mask somewhere in the tree. Ruined also.

I normally dressed and undressed myself, but right now I didn't care.

In fact, I think if I hadn't had Anna there, I would have simply collapsed on the bed and stayed there for a few days or maybe weeks.

Zachary had vanished. Just like Reed.

I remembered the way my sister Andrea had collapsed into shock when Reed had vanished right in front of her. At the time, I had sort of, but not quite understood what she was going through.

Now I knew. Now was having the experience myself.

But Zachary had not vanished in front of my eyes. Zachary had gone into the gazebo and had not come out.

I had asked several people if they had seen Zachary come

out of the gazebo. No one had. They had all seen me dancing with him, so I knew he was real, but no one had seen him come back inside after he'd gone into the fallen tree.

I must have made a sound. A cry or a groan. Something.

"Are you okay?" Anna asked.

"No," I said as she slipped my nightgown over my head. There was no way I was going back downstairs. Not now. Too many people. Too many questions.

"Your young man?" she asked.

Another sound. "Not my young man," I said, but without conviction.

The memory of Zachary's lips was imprinted on mine. I did not go around kissing random men. Perhaps that made him *my young man.*

Either that or I was a woman of ill-repute.

"Maybe," I said, not wanting to give Anna any fuel to scorch my reputation.

Anna smiled. "He's a handsome young man."

I nodded. "Yes. He is handsome."

Anna turned down the sheets. Took out the bed warmer she had placed at the foot of my bed beneath the blanket.

"He'll come back," she said as I sat on the edge of the bed.

"How do you know?"

She just shrugged. "I know men. Was married once."

She pulled the blanket up to my chin. Tucked pillows behind me.

"The war," she said. "I'll be right back with your hot water."

The war.

Two words that required no explanation. Everyone knew what it meant. Families had been torn apart. Lives shattered.

We had ended up out here, but even though the road had been rife with heartbreak, it had turned out well enough. For my two older sisters anyway.

For Bailey, better than well enough. She had a man who

loved her. A man who had the means for her to live like an empress.

Even to dress her sister like one, I thought with a rueful smile at the loss of my golden dress. As much as I had complained about wearing it, I secretly liked it.

And having met and danced with Zachary while wearing it, I liked the dress even more.

I picked up the dance card that had ended up on my nightstand and ran a hand across his signature.

He had claimed all my dances, but we had only danced one.

I had enjoyed dancing with him, but I had enjoyed being with him in the library even more.

After Anna brought hot water in a mug to warm me from the inside out, I let the steam warm my face and hands while I replayed that kiss.

Maybe Anna was right. Maybe Zachary would come back.

I had to keep up hope.

At any rate, Bailey could stop trying to find a husband for me.

I had found the only man I would even want to think about marrying.

CHAPTER 14
ZACHARY

*M*y boss was furious.

I had missed the fundraiser.

And since I wasn't there to spur them on, Hudson and Tiffany had delayed their decision making.

Things were even worse because I couldn't account for my time.

Hudson looked at me sideways whenever I walked past him.

How was I supposed to talk to him about a billion-dollar deal when he couldn't look me straight in the eye?

Since I wasn't getting anywhere here, I decided to take a drive into Whiskey Springs.

Dakota was from Whiskey Springs. I wanted to check it out.

As I drove my rented Mercedes into town, I found myself looking for her walking on the street.

It occurred to me that I hadn't seen her without a mask. I knew she had brunette hair, lush bow-shaped lips, but that was about it.

I was an idiot. A man driving along the streets of a little town looking for a woman he wouldn't even be able to recognize.

I shut that down and concentrated on the traffic, turned on the radio to listen to the local news.

That lasted for all about half a minute.

Until a brunette girl crossed the street in front of my car while I sat waiting for the light to turn green.

Nope. Too tall.

Dakota was the perfect height for me. Her cheek rested easily on my chest and her head tucked just beneath my chin.

One of the cars behind me honked.

I looked up at the green light and let out a curse word as I hit the gas pedal.

I didn't know where I was headed. Nowhere in particular. Just driving.

It was off-season, so there were only a few tourists out. A lot of the shops were even closed. I easily found a parking spot on Main Street, got out and started walking as aimlessly as I had been driving.

I went into a café. Ordered a burger and fries. Answered some email.

Tried to get Dakota out of my head. But she had hijacked my brain and I could not stop thinking about her. I should not have kissed her.

That was it. I broke one of my own rules. Don't play where you work. And I had been working.

It was just… the party… the gazebo… everything had gotten so blurred and confused. I gave myself a pass on it.

Spent some time looking up plane tickets from Denver to New York since I had missed my flight.

I needed to go out when I got back to New York. I had not been out in… well… forever.

I face-timed my buddy Eric before I changed my mind.

"You look like something the cat dragged in," Eric said.

"Good to see you, too," I said. "Hey. When I get back to the city in a couple of days, want to get together? Have a beer?"

"You look so serious. I'm supposed to be the serious one." Eric pulled a straight face. It usually made me smile, but I just wasn't in the mood.

"Been busy," I said.

"Okay, sure," Eric said. "Just call me when you get in. We'll go out. Hook up with a couple of girls."

"Sure thing. Later." I disconnected the call. Somehow the whole idea of going out and looking at, much less, making it with some girl who wasn't Dakota made me feel ill.

Maybe this was some kind of evolutionary thing the body did to make sure humans propagated. Made families.

Women needed to get pregnant and their men needed to stay near them. Take care of them. At least that's what the cave men had to do. And as much as we may disagree and think things were different, our bodies had some pretty strong ingrained DNA.

So that was it. My body knew I liked her. Had spurted out a bunch of hormones when I kissed her and here we were.

It would wear off.

I'd get back to New York and everything would go back to normal.

To my same dull, workaholic life.

I settled up my ticket and headed back out to the streets.

A bookstore caught my attention.

I took a deep breath. Let it out.

I wanted to buy Dakota a book. Something she might enjoy, even though I had no idea what that might be.

So I ducked into the bookstore and wandered around aimlessly, unsuccessfully trying to convince myself that I would never even see her again.

There was a fireplace, burning real wood, in the back of the store with a little sitting area.

How cool was that?

I took a seat. Did some deep breathing.

I liked it here. The store had great ambiance.

A woman, a clerk I'd seen up front, came and sat down next to me.

She held out a coffee-table looking book—hardcover with a nice blue toned cover on it.

"Give her this," she said. "she'll like it."

I took the book. "Who?"

"Dakota," she said. "It'll help her understand. Besides," she said with a kind smile. "It's a really nice book."

I looked at the cover. A lavender blue swipe across it with a simple title. *Auclair.* And a simple tagline. *Lavender Blue.*

My heart was beating far too fast and my hands were trembling as I carefully opened the cover and flipped through a few pages.

It was a book with pictures of Bailey Auclair's paintings.

I closed the book and looked at the woman more carefully now.

She wasn't a day over forty. She had a very serene, calm demeanor that put me at ease as I studied her.

"Why?... How?... I don't…"

"It's okay," she said with a little smile. "Let's just say I have my way. How and why really don't matter so much."

I shook my head.

"Do I know you?" I asked, recovering somewhat.

"You couldn't," she said. "You see I'm your great great aunt. Maybe great great great aunt. But too many greats on there make me feel old, so let's just say I'm your aunt."

"I don't have any aunts."

She held up a finger. "Ah ha. But your grandfather on your mother's side had a brother."

"I don't know. Maybe. I never kept up with the family history."

"You should always study history, Dear," she said. "You never know when you might have a use for it."

"What are you? My fairy godmother or something?"

She smiled. "You're quick on your feet. I like you."

I smiled and sat back. "Then, can you help me understand?" I lifted the book in my lap, put it back.

"I think I can. But first…" She held out a hand. "May I?"

I handed her the book, even though I found that I wanted to keep it.

She turned to a page in the back. Handed the book back to me.

"Take a look," she said.

My gaze on hers, I took the open book and held it in my lap.

It was illogical that I was feeling nervous.

She tapped a finger on the page.

I looked down. And right there was a photograph of Bailey Auclair.

"Does she look familiar?" the woman asked.

"Not really." But there was something familiar about her.

"Imagine her with a mask." The woman reached over, turned the page. "Like this."

A cold sweat washed over me. "I saw her."

"Yes. You did."

"That's. Not. Possible." I turned to the next page. "That was nearly two centuries ago."

"But you met. You stood in front of the fireplace with her. She wanted you to meet her sister."

I gaped at the woman sitting in front me for a moment, then went back to the book.

Studied the photos more carefully. I turned another page. *Family.*

There were photos of her children. Then on the other side, there were photos of her family of origin. Bailey's siblings.

I studied each one in turn.

When I saw *her*, my heart skipped a few beats.

I hadn't seen Dakota without her mask. But if I knew her even before I saw her name printed below her photo.

Dakota Auclair.

"Wait a minute," I said, shaking my head. "I met Bailey Daniels, not Bailey Auclair.

She tapped the page again, drawing my attention to the man in the photo next to hers.

Graham Daniels.

"Bailey was a little ahead of her time. She used her maiden name for her art."

I studied the photo of Dakota again.

Then I just sat back and grinned.

"This is crazy, right? You were at the party."

The woman shook her head. "No, Dear. I wasn't at the party."

She looked at me with what looked a little... a lot... like disappointment. "But you're smart. You'll figure it out."

She got up and, with a great deal of grace, walked toward a door in the back.

I blinked. I think.

And she vanished.

"What?"

Still holding the book, I followed her. The door wasn't locked, so I opened it and looked inside.

It was obviously a one-room office.

A matronly looking woman with glasses—no kindness on this woman's face—looked up. "No public restroom," she said.

"I don't—"

The woman lowered her glasses. Glared at me over them.

"Sorry," I said and stepped back out, closing the door.

Taking the book back to my chair, I sat down and started reading on page one.

CHAPTER 15
DAKOTA

*T*he snow had not lasted. The sun had come the next day and melted it all away.

That allowed all the guests to leave, driving their buggies and carriages down a muddy road. But at least they were driving them away from here.

I let the curtain fall from my second-floor window after the last of them left.

I had watched every one of them. Looking for Zachary.

But he was not among the guests who were leaving.

I spent the rest of the day rambling about the house by myself.

Bailey was resting as she should have been even last night. But my sister was a stubborn one.

I went up to her studio, sat at her desk, and opened to a fresh sheet of paper on one of her sketchpads.

Bailey was the artist, but all four of us girls had taken art. We were all decent enough.

I was feeling edgy. Restless.

I clearly remembered the time my oldest sister Andrea had sketched a picture of Reed. We had given her a terribly hard time about it, mostly because we knew she was crushing on him.

I wasn't all that good at landscapes like Bailey. I was mostly good at abstract painting, but I didn't feel right getting into my sister's paints without her here or at least her permission.

So I borrowed one of her charcoal pencils and sat tapping the paper. My thoughts were scattered.

Giving up and letting my mind wander, I sketched out the gazebo. The workers were supposed to come back tomorrow and fix it. Other than a broken glass door, it had fared okay considering a tree fell right against the front of it.

I added the fallen tree. Broken limbs. Glass on the ground.

Trees fell all the time. It was just odd that it had fallen right then and there. It was even odder that it fell right after Zachary kissed me.

I filled in some of the background. The tall, rugged mountains. So tall no one had ever been to the peaks.

Why had Zachary pushed his way into the gazebo?

Just as he had seemed to be looking for someone as we walked, he almost seemed like he thought there was someone in the gazebo he needed to rescue.

Very strange, I decided.

I started a general sketch of the man.

Time travel by its nature made very little sense.

I needed to talk to my sister.

I had been letting her rest today. To get over the exhaustion from the party.

But maybe it was time to seek her out. To find out what she knew.

My sister knew a thing or two about time travel.

I decided my sketch was good enough and leaving it there, went outside to get some fresh air.

The air was briskly biting. And as always, I failed to dress properly before going outside.

I was always forgetting to grab a cloak before going out the door.

I guess you could take the girl out of Mississippi, but it was harder to take the Mississippi out of the girl.

Leaning over the rail, I looked out over Whiskey Springs. A sleepy little town. But I could see just enough to know that people were moving around down there. A wagon here. A horse and rider there. Some people on foot.

It was comforting. I wasn't sure I would want to live up here all alone all the time.

It seemed like it would get lonely.

Of course, if I had someone like Bailey had.

If I had someone like Zachary.

Well then, it might just be okay.

I might even like it.

CHAPTER 16
ZACHARY

"We called your office," Tiffany said. "Asked for someone else to come out and work with us on the possible acquisition of our home."

I stood in the parlor of the Daniels house staring into the gas produced flames. Musing about how they had ruined these fireplaces when they replaced out the real logs. The ones that crackled when they burned and smelled like a cozy campfire.

Looking up at Tiffany, I kept my expression blank. I was already in a world of trouble at my job. This was not going to help.

"There's really no need to do that," I said, only half-heartedly.

She lifted a delicate brow that carried traces of her Auclair ancestors.

"Well, first you disappeared for two days." She crossed her arms. "Only to come back all bloody and disheveled. Then you drive off again. And now you're here, but… I honestly think there's something wrong with you."

I didn't disagree.

"I'm sorry," I said, looking back into the flames.

"That's it? No explanation?"

"I would explain if I could. I spent the today in Whiskey Springs trying to figure it out for myself.

"Well," she said. "You seem unstable. I wouldn't trust you to handle the sale of this house even if we decided to do it."

I laughed a little to myself. But it was enough to bring out her anger.

"I think you should go," she said.

"I think you're right," I said. But I had things that were unfinished. Like Dakota Auclair. "I'll go in the morning."

"Go now."

"I don't think so."

Hudson walked into the parlor. "What's going on?"

"Zachary is just leaving," Tiffany said.

"I'll leave in the morning."

"Tell him to go." She looked at her brother.

"Tif," he said. "Let the man leave in the morning."

"Fine," she said, turning in a huff and walking away.

"I'm sorry," I said again. "Something happened."

Hudson poured two glasses of bourbon. Handing me one.

"I think you should see a doctor," he said.

I took a sip. Looked at him over the glass.

"Think about it. You disappear for two days. Come back all shredded up. You lost time. You do know that's a disorder, right?"

"I did lose time," I agreed.

"See a psychiatrist," he said.

I leaned a hand against the mantle, holding my glass with my other hand.

"I will," I said.

If he knew about the woman I'd met in the bookstore, he really would think I needed to get help. The woman who knew things no one else knew, then just disappeared.

"I'll stay in my room until in the morning. Then I'll go," I said. This situation was going to cost me my job. I would put money on it.

What bothered me most was that I didn't care. For a man who had been driven and singularly focused on my career for all my adult life, there was something wrong that I wasn't bothered that I was about to be fired.

I downed the bourbon, nodded at Hudson, and went upstairs to my room.

I threw my things into my suitcase.

My toiletries, t-shirts, shoes.

I picked up the tux. Remembered that I was supposed to return it in town. If I'd been thinking, I would have returned it today.

I might as well keep it though. With the ripped sleeves, they were going to make me pay for it anyway.

On second thought, I tossed it in the suitcase.

Packed now and ready to go, I considered leaving tonight like Tiffany had asked.

I went to the nightstand. Picked up the book Lavender Blue.

I couldn't leave yet. I had something I needed to do.

But I would wait until night.

True to my word, I stayed in my room until just after Midnight.

I knew that Hudson and Tiffany would be asleep by then.

I had spent the time productively. I had spent it thinking and doing a little research on the Internet.

I found it telling, not that the Auclairs were looking for someone to handle their transaction—that had never happened to me before—but that I wasn't all that concerned about it.

In fact, I decided that it was time for me start my own company. I'd always had an entrepreneurial spirit, so it wasn't out of the blue.

I spent the time doing research on going out on my own.

Not much had changed in the few years since I last checked this out.

But back then I had been doing well enough working for a company, so I had stayed where I was.

Nonetheless, I had the skills. I had the personality. I had the drive.

What more could a man need?

The capital.

I had that, too.

By Midnight I had filled several pages notes on a legal pad.

I'd even done a little research on the history of marketing. Just out of curiosity.

I put on my coat, my gloves, my wool cap and quietly made my way downstairs.

The wind was startlingly cold. Should have checked the weather. But it didn't really matter right now.

Using my phone as a flashlight, I went around back of the gazebo, flipped the switch to turn on the heat inside.

Fortunately, it was an instant blowing heat, so it didn't take all that long to heat up the little gazebo.

It had overhead lighting, too.

This is where I had been when I had gone back in time.

Going back in time was the only logical explanation for what had happened to me.

I decided I would see about going back in time again. And this time I would bring Dakota home with me.

It seemed like an easy enough plan, even if it was a little bit crazy. Maybe a lot bit crazy.

The woman at the bookstore had suggested I give this book to Dakota.

That was all well and good, but I had to get to Dakota before I could give her anything.

CHAPTER 17
DAKOTA

I stood at the window, on the fourth floor of my sister's house.

It had been snowing for three days now.

If anyone wanted to go down the mountain to town, they would have to take a sled down the road. Which meant no one was going.

The only people who could get around in this of weather were the trappers. They had the right kind of boots. The right overcoats and gloves. They knew their way around.

It was so quiet when it snowed like this. The snow was like a blanket that settled silently over the earth.

With everything covered in snow that sparkled in the late evening sunlight, it looked like a winter wonderland. Untouched by human footsteps. Such pristine beauty.

I caught sight of an elk walking by, twitched its ears, leaving little footprints that were barely visible.

The animals were part of the scene. It was the humans that spoiled everything.

Bailey was sitting at her desk, playing around with one of

her sketches. She said she was trying something new, but hadn't told me what it was yet.

"Why don't you go downstairs?" she asked. "Play the piano?"

"Maybe later," I said. "I've got a book I'm reading right now."

She shrugged and kept sketching.

I pressed my forehead against the cold glass and fogged over a little spot with my warm breath.

I drew a heart in the mist. And wrote *Zachary* under it.

Then I watched it fade. Just like my dreams.

A movement from below caught my attention.

I stood on my toes and looked down. Five bighorn sheep walked in a line below making a trail in the snow between the back of the house and gazebo.

I don't know what I expected. Maybe I expected to see Zachary coming from the gazebo.

Fanciful.

I went back to my chair in front of the fireplace, tucked my feet beneath me, and picked up my book.

And just as I had done a million times, I replayed that evening I had spent with Zachary.

He had asked *what do you do*.

I had been trying to figure out what he meant.

When I heard Graham coming up the stairs a few minutes later, I decided to ask him.

I waited until after he kissed Bailey on the lips and looked at what she was working on—she almost always showed him her work even when she wouldn't show me.

"Graham? Can I ask you something?"

"Sure. What's up?" He knelt down and poked at the fire. Picked up a couple more logs and tossed them in.

"If someone, say a man, asks what you do, what kind of answer are they looking for?"

"It usually means they want to know what kind of job you do."

"A job?"

"Yeah. Who wants to know?"

"No one," I said. "It's okay. I just heard someone talking at the party."

Zachary wanted to know what kind of job I did.

That took me aback a bit for one simple reason.

I didn't do any kind of work.

If the tree hadn't fallen in that moment, what could I have told him?

I read a lot, studied some, played the piano.

But as for a job, why would he ask me something like that?

Maybe he thought I was a school teacher or a nurse or even a musician.

I decided he must have asked because of my golden dress. Maybe he thought I was an actress of some sort.

Or… maybe he thought I was an empress.

The thought made me smile.

I opened my book and went back to reading.

After supper, the three of us settled into the main parlor.

Bailey, always needing to be doing something, worked on her needlepoint.

Graham did some writing using one of Dakota's charcoal pencils or one of his own wooden pencils. I'd never seen him use a quill. I don't think he knew how.

I settled in with my book.

"Why don't you play the piano, Dakota?" Bailey asked.

"Yes, please." Graham added. "It's far too quiet around here tonight."

It was always quiet as far as I could tell, but I was happy to play.

In our house in Whiskey Springs, on a cold night like this, I could often hear piano music drifting from the nearby saloon.

At the time, we hadn't had a piano, so I had gotten used to not being able to play.

I ran my fingers over the elegant grand piano.

To me, it was a work of art. Almost too pretty to touch.

But I sat down on the shiny black bench anyway and arranged my skirts around me.

Once my fingers touched the keys, I forgot to worry about anything at all.

My fingers just went into memory mode and I started playing.

I put my heart into it, pouring out all the emotions I felt for Zachary.

CHAPTER 18
ZACHARY

I must have fallen asleep. It took me a couple of minutes to even figure out where I was. It was dark and it was cold.

I was sitting on the floor of the gazebo. I know I had been sitting in a chair.

It smelled different—like freshly sawn wood. And... unusually fresh clean air.

Quiet. No heaters or air conditioners roaring in the background.

It reminded me of a weekend I'd spent at a country estate in Alabama. They'd had a power outage. Just like this.

My brain registered all this in a flash before I let myself consider the possibility that I might have gone back in time.

A quick search told me I did not have my cell phone with me, so I had to function in the dark.

I stood up slowly, using the back wall to get my balance. I wasn't shivering, so I hadn't been out here in the cold for very long.

I thought I heard music, but I shook it off as my mind playing tricks on me.

Turning the knob and opening the door, I had to push hard against a bank of snow. Then I was blasted by a flurry of snowflakes.

We were right in the middle of a blizzard.

Since there was no way this much snow could have fallen since I came out to the gazebo, I dared believe that I might be in the past.

With my heart tripping a little too fast, I trudged through two feet of snow, my way lit only by moonlight. As I got closer and closer, I most definitely heard music. Piano music.

This was the house in the past. This was Dakota's time.

I could just tell. No signs of electric lights on the veranda as I made my way up the steps, knocking off snow as I went.

I stood staring at the closed door.

This was a most unusual situation.

I could knock on the door. *Hi. I'm Zachary. From the future.*

Instead, I paced down one side of the veranda toward the music.

The curtains were open, giving me a clear view of the inside of the house.

A lady sat at a grand piano in a candlelit room. I could only see her back and a glimpse of her profile as she played the piano with more heart and feeling than any pianist I had ever heard in concert.

I sat on the swing hanging on the other end of the veranda and closed my eyes, enjoying the music, freezing my ass off.

After about five minutes, I made the decision to just go all in.

I went to the door and knocked.

When no one came to the door, I knocked again.

A man who looked like a butler opened the door. He was a big man. Tall. Dressed all in black. Very formal.

"Good evening," the butler said.

"Good evening," I said, forcing my teeth not to chatter.

"Why are you out here?" he said, stepping aside. "Come in." That told me I was most definitely not in my own time. I was without a doubt in a past time. An innocent time.

"Thank you." I stepped inside the version of the house I instantly recognized.

"How can I assist you?" the butler asked. He was a fairly big guy and even though he had let me inside, there was no getting past him without his permission. I would not want to cross him.

"I'm here to call on Miss Dakota Auclair."

"Your name?"

"Zachary Rivers."

"Wait here," he said. "I'll let her know you're here. See if she's available."

I stood there in the back foyer of the huge four-story house and pulled my wool coat tighter. It was no doubt a lot of space to heat with fireplaces and that heat didn't reach this far.

I wouldn't call this a mud room. I'd call it a back door foyer. There were hooks with half a dozen heavy looking cloaks hanging on them. Boots. A couple of baskets.

Everything was very organized and clean.

The minimalist in me was impressed.

The piano music stopped and the house was quiet.

Then I heard footsteps.

"Can I take your coat?" the butler asked.

I shrugged, reluctantly, out of my coat and handed it to the butler. Then I handed him my hat and gloves

"Come with me," he said, draping my coat over his arm.

Running a hand through my hair to straighten it, I followed him down what I knew to be one of two halls. He led me to the library. The same library where I had kissed Dakota.

He stood aside for me to walk inside the room bright with candlelight and a blazing wood burning fireplace. A welcome heat after being out in the cold.

A beautiful young lady—no mask—sat, back straight, on a sofa. Her hands were clasped in her lap.

This was Dakota. Just like the picture.

She was more beautiful without her mask than I had dared imagine and more beautiful than in the picture.

The butler left us there, pulling the door to, not quite closing it.

I smiled.

She narrowed her eyes at me.

"Zachary Rivers," she said.

"Dakota Auclair."

A flutter of a smile crossed her features.

"Welcome back," she said.

"Thank you."

"You're welcome to warm yourself by the fire," she said.

"Is it that obvious?" I asked, but I moved to stand in front of the fire anyway, tucking the book beneath my arm.

"Your nose is quite red."

"It's cold outside," I said.

"I know you didn't come by way of the road." She kept her gaze on mine.

"Maybe I did."

She shook her head. "Not possible."

"Maybe I came via the gazebo."

She stared blankly at me.

Not the reaction I had expected.

Not disbelief.

Acceptance.

CHAPTER 19
DAKOTA

"What do you have there?" I asked, nodding in the general direction of what was obviously a book.

"A gift," he said. "for you."

"What is it?" I asked.

"May I sit next to you?"

"Of course," I said. I hated that he was being so formal. But I didn't know what to make of him and he likely didn't know what to make of me.

He sat next to me and placed the book in my hands.

Lavender Blue. Bailey Auclair.

"My sister," I said, looking up at him questioningly.

"Yes," he said. "Bailey."

Carefully opening the book, I flipped slowly through the pages. So many of Bailey's paintings, all with her titles and many with a date.

I recognized a lot of them. A lot them I didn't.

"Where did you get this?" I asked.

"Turn to the back," he said, watching me carefully.

Before I could react, he turned to the back for me.

There were photos in this book too. Pictures of my sister. Her husband. Our whole family together.

And me.

I turned another page. There was another picture of me and…

"That's you," I said.

"What?" He leaned over. "No. That's not possib—"

He took the book from me and flipped through the pages. Looking for something.

He suddenly closed the book.

"What is it?"

He looked away into the flames.

I put a hand on his arm, coaxing him to meet my gaze.

"Tell me," I said.

"It's different now," he said. Then he looked at me. "That picture wasn't there before."

"The one of you?"

"Yes."

"It doesn't make sense," I said. "Why would your picture be in there? In a book about Bailey?"

He didn't answer. Just gazed into my eyes. "You're beautiful," he said.

"And there's that charming tongue again."

"What do you have against a bit of charm?" he asked.

"A man with a silver tongue is not to be trusted," I said.

"And who told you that?" he asked.

"My mother," I said.

He laughed. "No wonder. Alright," he said. "I won't be charming anymore."

"I don't think you can help it," I said. "I think it's part of your nature."

"In that case," he said. "I don't stand a chance with you. Do I?"

I shook my head. "No," I said softly, but I was leaning

toward him. Just a little and he was leaning toward me. Just a little.

He lightly touched my chin. I closed my eyes and waited.

He kissed my forehead and released my chin.

I opened my eyes and straightened.

"I can't kiss you right now," he said.

"Why not?"

"Because you should not be kissing on men you don't trust."

I smiled. "You're right." I reached for the book. Opened it to the back. To the picture of me and Zachary.

Then I laughed out loud. I laughed so hard I had to put a hand over my mouth.

"What's funny?" he asked.

I took a deep breath. Forced myself to stop laughing.

"My sister put you up to this."

"Your sister? Bailey?"

"Yes."

"Why would she do that?"

"Because she is determined for me to be married." I shrugged. "And I guess she thinks you'll do."

"Can I see the picture again?" he asked.

I turned it so that he could look at it. I was trying desperately to keep a straight face.

Bailey was trying to play this off like it was fate or destiny.

She had had this book put together. Just so she could convince me that I was going to marry Zachary.

Zachary looked closely at the photo. Then looked at me.

"Did you read this?" he asked.

"I did read it."

"It says we're married."

"It's Bailey's doing," I insisted.

"Then tell me," he asked. "When was this picture taken?"

When indeed.

CHAPTER 20
ZACHARY

The book had changed.

I was absolutely, positively sure about it.

I had memorized everything about this book.

The book's copyright date was 2022. Dakota's photo was in the back.

Mine was not.

Now there was a photo of the two of us together.

Zachary Rivers and Dakota Auclair Rivers.

What kind of trick was this?

I would have said the picture was photoshopped, but the book had not left my possession.

Dakota seemed to think that Bailey had put this book together to convince her that she should marry me.

That was one of the craziest things I had ever heard.

Especially since I knew good and well that I had bought the book in the future.

"What year is this?" I asked. It was time to get to the bottom of this.

"1868."

"Right." I flipped to the front of the book. "See this copyright date. 2022. This book was put together in 2022."

Dakota just blew out a breath and turned away. "Bailey has enough money that she just had that made. They could put anything there."

She was right about that. Except they didn't.

"No," I said. "Dakota. Look at me."

She turned and faced my gaze. "I bought this book in the future. In a bookstore. With a credit card."

"What's a credit card?"

"Exactly. Unless your sister is some kind of sorcerer, she did not do this."

"Bailey's not a witch," she said.

"I don't think so either," I said, closing the book and setting it aside. "So that just leaves one explanation."

"What's that?" Dakota looked at me warily.

"When I came back in time, I changed history."

Now she was looking at me with narrowed eyes. And blatant disbelief.

"I can't marry you," she said.

"Why not?"

"Because you're from the future. And I just can't deal with that."

I laughed. "Why do you say you can't deal with it."

"Because Andrea's husband is from the future. They had to move to Denver. If he comes back to Whiskey Springs, he could go through a portal and go back to the future."

"Reed is from the future?" I was trying to absorb this information.

"Yes."

"And," she looked at me and lowered her voice. "I think Graham is, too."

"Bailey's husband, Graham?"

"Yes," she said. "But they don't know I know."

"Why not?"

"We don't talk about it.

"That seems like the kind of thing you would talk about."

"On the contrary," she said.

"Actually…" I said.

"Actually what?"

"Nothing."

Actually I needed to talk to Graham.

CHAPTER 21
BAILEY

*I*f my sister did put that book of her paintings together, she had gone to a lot of trouble for no reason.

I wasn't going to marry Zachary. He wouldn't even kiss me. He'd kissed me once and now he wouldn't kiss me again.

The kicker was I wanted him to.

Maybe I shouldn't have accused him of having a silver tongue. Of being a man who couldn't be trusted.

The truth was, I didn't know what to make of him.

He shows up. He vanishes. Then he shows up again.

For all I knew, he would simply vanish again. I looked at him sideways.

He was painfully handsome. Even more handsome without his mask than he had been with it. Even without it, I had recognized him immediately.

Something tickled the back of my brain, but I pushed it away.

Zachary found a decanter of whiskey and filled two glasses. He handed me one.

I sniffed it and wrinkled my nose, then I drank it anyway, draining the glass.

Zachary looked at me in disbelief.

"Did you just drink that?"

"Yes," I said.

He sniffed his own glass. "This is strong," he said. "Do you… drink… a lot?

"I never drink," I said.

He cursed under his breath.

"It's okay," I said. "It was just a little bit in the glass." But I was feeling a bit… light-headed.

"A little of this goes a long way," he said, setting his aside.

"Aren't you going to drink yours?" I asked.

"Not now," he said. "I'm your designated driver."

"My what?" My lips were feeling pleasantly tingly.

"A gentleman never drinks when his lady is drinking."

I grinned. "Am I your lady?"

"Yes," he said. "I think you are."

"Good," I said. "My lips are numb."

"I'm sure they are," he said. "Maybe you should lie down."

"I'm not sleepy."

"If you'll lie down, I'll rub your feet."

"That would be scandalous," I said. "You can't do that."

"Come on," he said. "Don't be afraid."

"I'm not afraid," I said, with a quick glance toward the door. "But…"

Then I remembered what I had been thinking about earlier. The thing that had been teasing the back of my mind.

If Zachary was going to leave anyway, no one ever had to know that he had kissed me. And no one ever had to know that he had rubbed my feet.

I could be positively scandalous with him. Then he would vanish. And I could go back to being myself.

"Okay," I said. "You can rub my feet."

"Here," he said, patting his knees. "Feet."

I put my feet in his lap.

"Get comfortable," he said.

So I did. I leaned back and closed my eyes.

This was probably going to get me into so much trouble.

But, I decided, my logic was sound.

Zachary slowly pulled off one of my boots, then the other, putting them on the floor.

It tickled, having him touch my bare feet.

And Oh. My. God. It felt so very good.

He massaged everything from my toes to the back of my ankles.

And I was so relaxed.

I felt so safe with him.

CHAPTER 22
ZACHARY

Dakota was going to get me shot. I'd read about how men of this time shot each other in duels for far less.

But I could not let her walk around intoxicated.

Now that would be dangerous to both of us.

So I opted for trying to get her to fall asleep. To sleep it off.

Turns out rubbing her feet was dangerous also.

I should never have touched her bare skin.

Now I wanted to kiss her again even more.

But it wasn't long before she fell asleep. So I had been right about that.

I just sat there, holding her feet.

I was in something of rough spot.

I had come here to this time through the gazebo. The only way for me to get back to my own time was back through that gazebo.

But I didn't want to go back without Dakota.

If I had to go back to my time, I wanted to take her with me.

But I couldn't just kidnap her and take her to my time.

I needed to… court her.

And that would take time.

I'd already broken so many rules of this time.

I'd kissed her. Rubbed her feet. And apparently I had managed to get her drunk without even trying.

I didn't know if her brother-in-law was going to shoot me outright or demand that I marry her.

I wouldn't mind marrying her.

I had, after all, come here to get her.

But I really didn't care to be shot, not even under the guise of a duel.

So what was I to do?

I decided I needed to talk to Graham.

Dakota said he was from the future. I could plead my case. Explain that I, too, was from the future.

And I was kinda stuck here. We were snowed in.

He might just lock me in the gazebo and wait for me to travel through time again.

So. I just couldn't tell him about the gazebo.

No one needed to know about that.

Not even Dakota.

She was smart though and she had probably already figured it out.

That was okay. It was okay if she knew.

I just wouldn't mention it again.

One of the candles went out, leaving us in shadows.

I gently moved her feet aside and stoked the fire. Added a piece of wood from the wood bin

When I went back to the couch, she was curled up on her side, sleeping soundly.

Maybe now was a good time to go in search of Graham.

I stepped into the hallway, but someone had put out all the candles, leaving it dark.

That meant that Graham was most likely already gone to bed.

What was I supposed to do now?

Going back into the library, I picked up the *Lavender Blue* book and flipped to the back where the pictures of Bailey's family were.

I was there. Plain as day.

So that's how it worked. I'd gone back and added myself to history.

Maybe I'd even created a different timeline.

It was fate. I had to believe that.

I'd always thought that everything happened for a reason.

So if I was here, then I was meant to be here.

It was odd. Two of Dakota's sisters had married men from the future.

So maybe that was her fate as well. Maybe it was her fate to marry a man from the future.

I didn't know Graham or Reed, so I didn't know if there was a connection there. Maybe the Auclair family was the connection and us men were just happenstance.

Deciding I was thinking too much, I took a sip of my whiskey.

I wouldn't drink it though. I'd promised to be her designated driver.

I wanted to be her everything.

I couldn't explain it. It was just quite simply there.

A pull I had never felt before.

A certainty even.

CHAPTER 23
DAKOTA

"*D*akota, wake up."

I shook my head, not wanting to open my eyes.

But he wouldn't stop talking.

"Dakota. Anna is looking for you."

"Anna?" My eyes flew open. Anna, the lady in waiting.

But instead of Anna, I saw Zachary.

I sat up. "Zachary." Tried to straighten my hair. "Why are you—?" Then I remembered. And I felt the heat as it spread across my cheeks.

Wiggling my toes, I saw that my feet were still bare.

"Anna is here. Looking for you," Zachary said again. "You didn't go up to bed."

"Where is she?"

"She's waiting in the hallway."

I grabbed my boots and jumped up to follow Anna.

It was late. That meant Anna had waited up for me. I hadn't gone to bed because Zachary was here and he had rubbed my feet until I fell asleep. That had been after I'd drank the bourbon.

Stopping, I turned. Looked at Zachary standing there.

"Where will you…?"

"I'll sleep here on the couch," he said. "Just go."

It didn't seem right leaving him here alone, but I couldn't stay with him. Already I was skirting on the edge of impropriety.

And Anna really was waiting for me. She stood at the bottom of the stairs. Patiently waiting.

"You didn't have to wait up for me," I said.

"I was worried when you didn't come up to bed, Miss," she said. "I was going to leave you, but Mister Zachary asked me to wait. To take you to bed."

"Oh." That explained a lot. Anna often checked on me before she went to bed herself, but she had never waited up for me. Never had to. "It's okay, Anna," I said.

The grandfather clock chimed eleven times as we walked upstairs. It wasn't all that late, everything considered.

Anna stoked the fire while I changed into my nightgown.

She already had my bed warmed by the bedwarmer. If I stayed here much longer, I would start to get used to having a lady in waiting. That would not be a good thing to become accustomed to.

I climbed into bed and Anna left.

I lay very still beneath the warm blankets, staring into the darkness.

Zachary had come back from the future. Had that been intentional? He didn't seem distressed about it. I think if I found myself in another time—an unfamiliar time with unfamiliar people—I would be quite distressed.

The fire crackled and logs settled, sending embers up the chimney.

The first time I was fairly certain Zachary hadn't known that he was in the past. This time he knew. He had brought a book with him from the future.

I had laughed it off at the time, but I shouldn't have. I should have listened to him. Taken him seriously.

He claimed that the future changed by him coming back.

There was a picture of us together, but he and I had not taken a photograph together.

Even Bailey couldn't produce something like a photograph that hadn't been taken.

I needed to see it again.

But the book was downstairs in the library.

Unable to stay in place, I climbed out of bed, went to my wardrobe, and pulled out a light-weight fur-lined cloak that I sometimes wore inside the house on cold days. I slid my feet into some slippers and left my room.

The hall was in shadows with only a couple of candles left burning for light, but I knew the way well enough.

I hurried down the stairs and turned to make my way to the library.

It was possible that Zachary had already left. I hadn't exactly been welcoming toward him. On the contrary.

I pushed open the library door and peeked inside, but the curtains were pulled closed and the room was in darkness with just the banked embers of the fireplace for light.

I stepped inside anyway, giving my eyes time to adjust to the darkness. When they didn't, I went back out to the hallway and took a candle from a sconce on the wall.

Zachary was not here.

Nor was the book.

I sat down hard on the couch.

He had decided then. To not stay.

But how did one just decide they wanted to travel through time?

How did it work?

For Reed, it was walking through the front door of the

house in Whiskey Springs. For Graham... I didn't know what it was.

I needed to talk to Graham.

But that would have to wait until morning.

CHAPTER 24
ZACHARY

"*B*enson said you wanted to see me," Graham said, walking into the breakfast room where I sat.

Benson, the butler, who had been kind enough to offer me breakfast.

The snow had stopped falling and bright morning sunlight streamed in through the large window. Outside the ground was covered in a white pristine blanket.

I sat at the breakfast table having a cup of coffee while I waited for Benson to come back.

"Yes," I said, studying Graham. He was dressed like a man of the nineteenth century, but even if Dakota hadn't already told me that he was from the future—my time perhaps—I think I would have suspected it.

I couldn't say how, exactly. I just knew. Maybe it took one to know one.

As he sat across from me, Benson handed him a cup of coffee.

"Thanks, Benson," he said, but kept his gaze on mine.

"I'll just cut to the chase," I said, purposely using modern language. "I'm here to hang out with Dakota. I'd say to date her, but in my book that involves going out."

Graham sipped his coffee as he studied me. "And you arrived last night."

"Yes."

"You arrived in the middle of a snow storm with impassable roads."

"So it seems."

He nodded and seemed to consider.

"And you want to date her."

I shrugged, trying to hide my nervousness. If I was wrong about Graham being from the future, I wasn't sure what the consequences would be. "Would say dinner and a movie, but... you know."

"We have a media room on the fourth floor."

"A media room?" I asked. Perhaps I had been sorely mistaken in thinking I had gone back in time.

Graham shook his head and tried to hide a smile. "Not really," he said.

I forced myself to close my mouth. Graham had beaten me at my own game.

"What year?" he asked.

"2022."

"Where?"

"New York."

Benson set plates piled high with eggs, bacon, and hash browns in front of us.

"You?" I asked after Benson had left.

"Same year. Pittsburgh."

"Small world," I said, taking a bite of scrambled eggs, enjoying my own wit.

"Why Dakota?" he asked.

"Why Bailey?"

He nodded slowly.

"What do you want to know?"

"I think I know why," I said. "Dakota. But… why time travel? Why me?"

"You haven't met Vaughn Becquerel then," he said.

"The only woman I met recently had me buy a book of Bailey's art."

"Can I see it?"

"Sure," I said, taking the book from the chair beside me and handing it to Graham.

He flipped through it, quickly making his way to the back to the photos.

"You're in here," he said.

"I know. But I wasn't until last night."

"Interesting," he said. "Tell me about the woman."

"Pretty. Elegant. Knew things she shouldn't. Said she was my great great aunt. But didn't tell me her name. The she just walked off. Vanished."

"Sounds like Vaughn Becquerel," he said.

"Is she a witch or something?" I asked.

"Not like that."

Benson refilled our coffee cups. Dropped off some buttered toast.

"You could say Vaughn is the original time traveler. It started with her."

"She didn't tell me."

"Guess this is how she let you know. She knew I would tell you."

"I'm listening."

"I'll give you the abbreviated version. She left France in the 1700s. A mail order bride or such. They were trying to get respectable brides for the people of the colonies and she was one. Raised in a convent.

"Her traveling party was attacked by Indians and she was the only one who survived."

He stopped talking a minute. Sipped his coffee and bit into a bite of toast.

"A man, a Druid, I think, cast a spell to save her life. I'm telling you more than she told me. I've done some research."

"Okay." I sat, not touching my food now.

"The spell sent her through time. A rip in time. But the rip in time never healed. Quoting her now. People of her blood may also travel through time."

"Her descendants."

"Exactly. And the Druid added in a love spell."

"A love spell." I almost laughed, but Graham sounded serious.

"Time travel is not an exact science, but somehow it only seems to work when its purpose is to bring together two people who are meant to be together."

"So you're telling me that there is a time travel spell in her blood. Our blood. One that has been passed down from generation to generation like... DNA?"

"It brought me to Bailey. And a fellow named Reed to their oldest sister."

"And you think it brought me to Dakota."

"Do you?"

I thought about how I hadn't been able to think about anything but Dakota since the first time I had seen her. How I had come back here with the intent of taking her back to my time.

"It's very possible," I said. "I was...um..." I glanced over my shoulder and lowered my voice. "I was hoping to take her back to the future with me."

"No," Graham said, shortly. "You won't. It doesn't work like that. She doesn't have Vaughn's blood so she can't go through time. If you want to be with her, then you have to stay here."

CHAPTER 25

DAKOTA

I woke in my own bed, later than usual. One of my sister's ladies in waiting, probably Anna, had come in already and opened the curtain, letting in the morning sunlight.

The snow had stopped falling, but even before I looked out the window, I knew it had left behind a blanket of snow covering the ground.

My first thought before I even opened my eyes was Zachary.

Where was he? Was he still here? Or had he gone back to some unknown place in the future?

I took care getting dressed. Put on a pretty emerald day dress with a bow that tied in the back, the ties falling almost to the floor.

Like all the dresses my sister had commissioned for me since I got here, it was fancier and more elegant than my usual day dresses. Back in Whiskey Springs, I probably would have called it a ball gown. It looked more like one of Bailey's riding habits, actually, I considered as I studied my reflection in the full-length mirror.

I decided to leave my hair down after brushing it out a hundred times. Wasn't sure why, but our mother had ingrained that little habit in all of us girls. One hundred times in the morning. One hundred times before bed.

I realized I was stalling. It was odd because I wanted to see Zachary, but I didn't know if he was still here.

If he was, I decided, I would try to be less difficult with him.

But my mission this morning was set. I needed to talk to Graham.

It was a conversation I had never had with him.

I found him in his study on the first floor. He had a study on the fourth floor, too, where he could be near Bailey, but in the mornings before she got up, he often stayed downstairs and worked on his accounts.

I could only imagine that a man as wealthy as Graham had lots of accounting. And he did it all himself, too. He didn't allow anyone else in his financial business. Not even Bailey, as far as I knew.

"Come in," he said, after I knocked on the door.

I went straight to the chair in front of his desk and sat down.

"I need to talk to you," I said.

"Seems I'm popular today," he said. "What's up?"

I hesitated. Now that I was here, I wasn't sure if maybe I should have talked to Bailey first.

"Is this about Zachary?" he asked.

"You know about him? How?"

He closed the ledger he had been working on, using a pencil. Never ink.

"I know that he's here."

"Do you know how he got here?" I asked.

"Not in detail, no," Graham said, watching me warily.

He wasn't going to tell me anything, I decided. I was just going to have to jump right in there.

"I think he's from the future," I blurted. "Like Reed. And you." Now that I'd started, I couldn't stop. "Do you know where the portal is?"

"I think we need to back up for a minute," Graham said. "What makes you think Zachary is from the future?"

"He told me. And he showed me the book. A book with Bailey's drawings. And a photograph of him in it. Him and me. Together."

Graham leaned forward on his elbows. "Dakota," he said. "I'm going to tell you a story about a young girl from France."

"What does she have to do with Zachary."

"Everything," he said.

Then he proceeded to tell me the story of a young girl named Vaughn Becquerel who came over from France to marry a man she had never met.

And from there she traveled through a rip in time that saved her life.

People who carried her blood down through the ages traveled through time to find their soulmates.

I hung on his every word. And I knew.

Zachary had traveled through time to be with me.

And I dared to think that maybe, just maybe we were soulmates.

CHAPTER 26
ZACHARY

I sat in an oversized armchair in front of the fireplace on the fourth floor of the house.

It was my favorite room in the whole large house. The views of the mountain peaks and valleys below were unparalleled.

And the huge fireplace right in the middle of the room, that burned real wood in this time period, was warm and cozy.

My conversation with Graham had left me with so many things to think about.

He dashed all my plans. My plan to take Dakota back to the future with me. Once there, I would start my own company, get a house, and start a family. Not necessarily in that order. Maybe all at once.

But none of that was going to happen.

If I wanted Dakota, I had to stay in the past. To stay here.

I'd always considered myself a modern, contemporary man. I lived in Manhattan, for God's sake.

But in the future, my life—this life in the past—had already been lived. I would have died a long time ago. Centuries ago.

I poked at the fire with an iron poker and watched the sparks that drifted up the chimney.

Did it matter whether I lived in the past or the future? Life was still life. Whenever it was lived.

If I went back to the future without Dakota, I would not be happy. I knew that.

And if I were honest with myself, even going back with her would not necessarily ensure my happiness. I had all but burned my life down around me back there.

And it had all been for Dakota, hadn't it?

All I had to do was to wrap my head around living in the past for the rest of my life.

There was always the gazebo. But Graham had said something about not counting on the portal working after a certain amount of time had passed.

I didn't know if that was true, or just something he chose to believe. Either way, for me it would be a permanent decision. If I decided to stay here and make Dakota my wife, then I would stay here for the duration.

Already my photograph was in a book. So time itself had accepted me being here.

At first I thought she was a vision, but it was Dakota wearing a long emerald green dress, walking toward me.

Time wasn't the only thing that had accepted me being here.

My heart had accepted me being here.

Now there was just the minor detail of getting Dakota to accept it.

"Hi," I said.

"Good morning." She sat in the chair next to mine. "Graham said I would find you up here."

"I needed some time to think."

"How's that going for you?" she asked with a little smile. "The thinking?"

"I'm making some progress," I said.

She smoothed her skirts. "I talked to Graham, too."

"Then I guess we both know a little about what's going on," I said.

"I guess." She looked at me with her deep green eyes. Eyes that a man could fall into.

"What are we going to do?" I asked.

"I think that all depends on you," she said, a little smile on her lips. "You're the traveler."

"Yes," I said, looking away. "I was. But it's a decision I think we need to make together. I have some things I need to tell you."

An eagle flew past, his wings wide, soaring on the wind.

I took the sight of an eagle as a good sign.

CHAPTER 27
DAKOTA

*F*rom my experience with having a brother, I knew that when a man went off by himself to think, it usually meant he was in the midst of making a serious decision.

Graham had given Zachary permission to use the fourth floor, Bailey's studio, as his place to think. It wasn't like he could take a walk in the several feet of snow that surrounded the house.

Still, Bailey's studio was private and for Graham to offer it meant that he, too, thought that whatever Zachary was thinking about was serious.

After breakfast, I had spent some time pacing before I became impatient. Patience had never been my strong suit and I never claimed it was.

So I busted in on Zachary's private thinking time. I figured it must have something to do with me anyway, so I might as well have my input or at the least get an idea of what he was thinking.

"What is it you need to tell me?" I asked.

"I had a good paying job back in the future," he said with a quick sweep of his gaze around the room. "But here I have nothing."

"I don't—"

"Wait," he said. "When I say nothing, I mean the clothes on my back. I can't provide for you like this. We'd be doing good have some kind of shelter over our heads."

"Okay," I said. "You have no means."

He looked at me blankly for a moment. Then nodded.

"That's right. No savings. No family money. But in my favor, I can work. I'd like to start a business, but if that doesn't work out right away, I can do other things."

"What other things?" I asked.

He blew out a breath. "Not sure. I can do accounting. Things like that."

"When you asked me what I did," I said. "I didn't even know what you meant. I don't have any skills really either."

"You can play the piano."

"Would you have me working in a saloon then?" I asked with an impish smile.

"Not a chance," he said.

We looked at each other a minute.

I decided that while he was being honest, I'd be honest, too.

"I've never had to work. I have enough money to live on. So I think we would be okay."

"I don't know, Dakota," he said. "I'm not sure I'm cut out to be a kept man."

I laughed. "It would give you time to get your own business going, right?"

He nodded slowly. "So you're thinking maybe I should stay?"

"I'm saying that if you do, then we would not starve. Or have to live in a hovel."

"Alright. So we got that out of the way."

"Yes. We did. Now what?"

"I suppose now we need to see if the Vaughn Becquerel theory is right."

"We have to figure out if we're soulmates," I said. "How do we do that?"

"I guess we have to spend time together until we figure it out."

"Alright then," I said.

I didn't tell him, but I didn't have to spend time with him to figure out if he was my soulmate.

I already knew.

CHAPTER 28
ZACHARY

*T*here were some definite advantages to being an independently wealthy man from the future.

I was quickly learning what some of those things were.

Graham declared pizza night, gave the cook some time off, and the four of us gathered in the kitchen.

Having lived in New York for much of my adult life, I had eaten a boatload of pizza. But I could honestly say that I had never made one.

We sat around the kitchen table with flour, olive oil, yeast, and shredded cheese.

I soon learned that if Graham couldn't find something, he would have it made. Like the round pizza pans. He'd had them special made.

"What do we do with it?" I asked, looking down at the little pile of dough on the table in front of me. Graham had mixed it all up before giving each of us a little glob of dough.

I found it interesting that instead of using bowls, they just used the table itself as their work station.

Dakota smiled. "Knead it," she said. "Like this." She got right in there and started kneading her dough with her fists.

I followed her example. Getting mine kneaded into a ball like hers.

Sort of.

She looked over at mine. And hid a smile.

Mine was rather misshapen compared to hers.

"I'm used to eating pizza, not making it," I said.

"Don't worry," Bailey said, "You'll get the hang of it."

I must be in an alternate reality. Having THE Bailey Auclair, famous artist, and her sister, the most beautiful girl in the history of time, teaching me to make homemade pizza. But they were all being quite informal. An intimate, informal pizza night at the Auclairs.

"Do this," Dakota said, cupping her ball of pizza and carefully rolling it in her hands.

There was something oddly erotic about this, but I quickly tamped that down and focused on the task at hand.

Next, we each took a glass, turning it on its side, and used it to roll out our crusts. I mostly used my hands, except when Dakota was watching.

"Now everybody gets their own pizza pan," Graham said. The cast iron pans were surprisingly heavy.

"Why does it have to be round?" Bailey asked.

Graham and I looked at each other, then at her with similar appalled expressions.

"Because it's pizza," I said. "It's an American icon."

She just shrugged.

Graham opened a glass of wine while we waited for our crusts to rise.

I handed Dakota her glass. Leaned close. "Drink it slowly. It's supposed to be sipped."

She just grinned.

I kinda liked it that we had a secret between us now. No one else knew what we were talking about.

We each got to choose our own toppings for our own

pizzas. We had tomato sauce from a jar. Little pieces of chopped ham. And grated mozzarella cheese.

I was impressed.

"We usually have green peppers, fresh tomatoes, and basil, but not this time of year," Graham told me.

I looked over to see what Dakota was doing with her pizza toppings.

She had used the ham, tomato sauce, and cheese to design her pizza toppings into what looked amazingly like an American flag.

"What are you doing?" I asked on a little laugh.

"You said it was an American icon," she said. "I wanted mine to be all American."

"We should take a pict—" I stopped. "You should sketch that. To remember it by."

"I'll remember," she said. "But I can sketch it for you if you like."

"I would like that," I said. "very much."

Dakota was quick-witted, smart, and charming.

I wasn't complaining about spending time with her. Not in the least.

But I already knew my answer about being soulmates.

I had known my answer since the very beginning.

CHAPTER 29
DAKOTA

I was pretty sure that Zachary was never going to make it as a pizza chef. He had admitted that he was a consumer of pizza. Not a maker of it.

After wiping down the table, someone brought out plates and we ate dinner there.

Zachary ate his whole pizza and part of mine.

"You're a good eater," I said.

"I'll take that as a compliment," he said.

"As it was intended."

We sat in the parlor. Bailey and Graham sat side by side on one of the couches working on one of Bailey's needlework projects. He held her yard in his hands.

"What do we do now?" Zachary asked.

It seemed to be a question he was asking me a lot.

"We can do anything we want to do," I said. "We can read. We can play music. Or we can just sit and talk."

"I'd love to hear you play the piano again," he said. "But just talking sounds like a good idea."

"Agreed," I said.

"What are your other sisters like?" he asked.

"Thinking about trading me in already?" I asked, teasingly.

"Not on your life," he said. "Just curious. I'm an only child, remember?"

I settled on the couch, my feet pulled up beneath me to keep them warm. "Right. Well. My oldest sister is serious and responsible."

"I thought that was you."

"No," I said. "I'm the suspicious one."

"Really? That explains some things."

"Ha. Anyway my youngest sister, Elise is… sweet and innocent."

"Definitely not you," he said with a straight face.

I put a hand on his arm and playfully pushed at him.

"I have a brother, too," she said. "So you have to be nice to me."

"Colton, right?"

"Right."

"What's he like?"

"Colton is just Colton. He's the middle child, but he has lots of friends, you know. We don't see him all that much, unless we need him. Then he's right there."

"That makes for a good brother."

"Yes. It's too bad you don't have any siblings."

"Yeah, well." He tipped his glass and drained it.

"Not my designated driver tonight?" I asked.

"No, you seem to be pacing yourself much better. And you have your sister and Graham to take care of you if I can't."

"You're so responsible. Like my sister Andrea."

"I guess I am." I'd always been responsible in my work. At least until I wasn't. I wasn't so sure I was responsible in other aspects of my life. "I don't visit my parents like I should," I confessed.

"They're the ones who moved away, right?"

"Right."

"Then you can't beat yourself up over it. You can't do what everyone else wants you to do. You have to do what you want to do."

"Are you making a case for me to stay here with you in the past?" he asked.

"Maybe." I twirled my hair, feeling a bit flirty.

"Are you intoxicated again?" I asked, checking out her wine glass.

"I am not," she said with indignation.

"Good. It doesn't suit you."

"Is that so?"

"You're too close to your sister," he said.

"I don't think that's possible," I said. Then looked at him. "What do you mean?"

"I don't mean anything," he said. "Just maybe we could take a walk?"

"Outside?" I asked, frowning into the cold darkness.

"How about we just walk to the fourth floor?"

"Okay," I said, getting to my feet and holding out a hand.

The way I saw it, if he was auditioning to be my boyfriend, then he should go all out.

CHAPTER 30
ZACHARY

*W*alking through the shadows of the house hand-in-hand with Dakota seemed like we were doing something we shouldn't.

But I wanted nothing more than to be alone with her.

Graham and Bailey didn't seem to be paying us any attention and I doubted they even noticed when we left.

I was pretty sure they already knew that we were going to get married.

After all, a man didn't travel centuries back in time just for a one-night stand.

At least, that is, if he had any say about it.

The fourth-floor studio was lit only by moonlight, but it had so many windows it seemed to be enough.

I got the fire going and we sat in front of it.

"I don't know about this," I said.

"You don't know about what?" Dakota asked, her brow furrowed.

"You're too far away. Is there a blanket?"

"There's a fur blanket," she said, not moving.

"Where is this fur blanket? I'll get it."

"I think it's over in one of Bailey's storage wardrobes."

"Are you falling asleep?" I asked, getting up to look for the fur blanket.

"Maybe," she said.

Well, I thought to myself. I'll just have to fix that.

I found the fur blanket and spread it out in front of the fireplace.

"How's that?" I asked.

"It looks comfortable," she said.

"Come on." I held out a hand. "Sit with me."

We settled onto the blanket, side by side.

"This is better," I said.

She shrugged a little, keeping her gaze on the flames.

"Is something bothering you?" I asked.

"Not really." Then she turned and smiled up at me from beneath her lashes, a little pout on her lips.

"You have to tell me or I can't possibly know," I said. This woman was going to drive me insane.

"If you're going to be my boyfriend," she said. "Then it seems like you ought to kiss me."

I grabbed her arms and tipped her onto her back. I took her hands in my mine and held them loosely captive over her head.

"Your wish is my command," I said, then crushed my lips to hers.

She sighed beneath me and I nearly came undone.

"Better?" I asked, nuzzling one of her ears.

"I... um... I..."

I grinned to myself.

"I'm not sure," she said. "I think you need to do it again."

I obliged, my lips claiming hers, wrapping my arms around her. She wrapped her arms around me, toying lightly with my hair.

This was going to be even better than I could have ever imagined.

Dakota Auclair was the perfect woman.

CHAPTER 31
DAKOTA

*T*he next morning, it was snowing again. Not a heavy blizzard snow, but a light, feathery snow falling silently on the already snow covered ground.

Benson was baking something. Something sweet. Muffins maybe.

Still warm under the blankets, I stretched and smiled. My lips were still swollen from Zachary's kisses.

We'd kissed and kissed. Neither of us able to stop for what seemed like hours.

I had just finished brushing my hair out one hundred strokes when Anna came to my door.

"Mister Zachary is waiting for you downstairs," she said.

"Waiting? Why?" I set my brush aside and stood up.

"I'm not sure," she said, "But he said to wear something warm."

"Will this do?" I asked, sweeping a hand over my light blue dress.

"Hmm," Anna seemed to consider, then went to my wardrobe. Flipped through my dresses. "I think something more like this." She pulled out a heavy wool dress in shades of brown. With lots of layers.

"And…" she said, pulling out some thermals. "You should wear these."

"He said we're going outside?" I asked, getting undressed again.

"He said something about it," Anna said, helping me step out of the dress.

As much as I didn't want to, I knew I was going to miss Anna after I went home.

A few minutes later, I was dressed in enough layers to keep an iceberg warm.

Wondering what Zachary had in mind, that might require me to dress warm enough for a hike in the snow, I made my way downstairs.

The grandfather clock chimed the hour. Ten o'clock.

I went straight to the breakfast room. By the time I was sitting, Benson brought my hot coffee.

"Good morning," Zachary said.

I turned and smiled at him.

It seemed like forever since I had seen him, though it had only been a few hours.

It seemed I couldn't get enough of him.

"Good morning."

"Did you sleep well?" he asked, sliding into the chair next to mine. He swept his fingers through my hair under the guise of tucking a strand behind an ear.

"I slept so well, it seems I slept in. Have you been up long?"

"I've been up since dawn," he said.

"Why so early?"

"So much to think about," he said, smiling into my eyes.

Benson brought my breakfast. "I'll have fresh muffins out shortly," he said.

"Benson makes the best muffins," I said, biting into a piece of toast. "So that's what you've been doing. Just thinking for hours?"

"Mostly," he said. "Took a walk outside with Graham."

"Outside?" I shivered.

"Yes. And I want to show you something."

"I dressed warmly as asked," I said, sweeping a hand over my wool skirt.

"Warm and very fetching," he said, kissing me on the cheek.

I grinned and put a bite of toast in his mouth.

"You're like a little bird," I said.

"I'll be your bird if you'll be mine."

I laughed. "You're silly."

"Happy," he said. "I'm just happy as a lark."

As was I, I realized.

I was happier than I had ever been.

CHAPTER 32
ZACHARY

I walked hand-in-hand with Dakota in the softly falling snow. We were both wrapped up like turtles. Gloves on our hands. Thick wool scarves around our faces.

The sun reflected off the snow-capped mountain peaks across the valley. The lakes, untouched by man, were frozen.

Reaching a little overlook, we stopped and sat on a boulder.

The bitingly cold wind whipped over us, making our eyes sting.

A herd of bighorn sheep, maybe a hundred of them, grazed along the steep mountainside below.

"Oh my God," Dakota said. "They're beautiful."

She looked up at me. "How are they here?"

"They're rugged, I guess," I said.

"I've never seen anything like it."

"I haven't either."

"My sister should come here. She could paint this."

"I know, but Graham won't let her. In her condition and all. You can do it though."

"I'm not the artist."

"Don't sell yourself short," I said. "I've seen your drawings."

"I wish I could just take a picture of them and keep it forever. Like the photos in the book."

"It won't be too many years from now when people do that all the time. They just pull a camera out of their pocket, aim, and snap."

"Wow. The future must be an awesome place."

"This is pretty awesome, too, though."

I slowly and carefully unwrapped the scarf protecting my face, then tied it loosely so it wouldn't blow away.

Then I did the same for her.

I pressed my lips solidly against hers and just held them there. Letting the biting wind sweep around us at what felt like a hundred miles an hour while we were in our own little bubble.

"I'm not going anywhere," I whispered against her lips.

I felt her smile. Then kissed her again.

"So will you?" I asked. "Marry me?"

"Is this a proposal?" she asked, shivering.

"Let's call it a preliminary proposal."

"Then preliminarily yes."

I kissed her again.

"We're going to get frostbite," I said, quickly wrapping her scarf back around her. Then my own.

I stood up. Held out a hand. "Ready?" I asked.

With one last look at the bighorn sheep, she nodded and put her hand in mine.

I'd known all along, but this seemed like a beautiful place to tell her and to let her known my intentions.

A place and time neither one of us would ever forget.

As we walked back through the snow toward the Daniels mansion that one day in the future would probably become a hotel, I considered what Graham had told me.

He told me the house was built off unfortunate insurance payments. He taken the money from the airplane crash that had killed his entire family, including his fiancé, on his wedding day, and turned it literally into little gold nuggets.

He'd brought that gold with him to the past.

He told me in confidence. Not that there was anyone I could tell who would believe me.

He'd told me because he wanted me to know how he had gotten where he was. How he became independently wealthy.

I, the supposedly savvy business man that I was had not thought to do anything like that. In my defense, I had come to take Dakota home with me. Not to stay.

I think Graham told me so that I would know that if I did marry his sister-in-law, we would be taken care of.

I appreciated that, but I wanted to do it myself. Not to depend on someone else.

Graham was outside filling a row of bird feeders I hadn't noticed before. Painted in white, they sort of just blended in, but the birds found them.

"Need some help?" I asked as we passed.

"No. But thanks. Bailey wants to make a painting of the chickadees."

I looked up. Saw the very pregnant Bailey watching us from her own fourth-floor perch.

Graham, one of those men who doted on his wife, was a good role model for a man in any time period. Past or future.

CHAPTER 33
DAKOTA

*G*raham had put up a row of bird houses—he called it bird condominiums—with a sign Bailey had painted standing in the ground next to it. *Chickadee Café.*

"Actually," Graham said as we trudged through the snow where he was filling the bird feeders. "Would you hand me that bucket of bird seed?"

He'd brought two buckets outside and had emptied one of them. The snow was a bit difficult to walk through and was getting worse. I had a feeling we had just taken our last outing for a while.

"I'll be right back," Zachary said, kissing me on one of the few spots of exposed skin, right next to my eye.

"I'll wait," I said.

While I waited, I turned around and looked back the way we had come. We had broken the pristine blanket of snow, leaving behind a trail of footprints.

It wouldn't be long though before it was filled in again.

The snow was falling a little heavier now. And the wind had picked up. I was glad we had gone to see the bighorns, but I was ready to get back inside now.

The wind was strong enough that it swirled snow up off the ground and sprayed it through the air.

I'd ask Benson to make us some hot chocolate, then Zachary and I could sit in front of the fire again.

Maybe there would be kissing.

I smiled to myself beneath my scarf.

Zachary was staying. He was staying and we were going to get married.

I hadn't planned on getting married, but sometimes it just happened.

Blinking against the biting wind hitting my face and turned, looking up at my sister. She looked like a very pregnant princess in her tower.

Except this princess had a paint brush in one hand and a canvas in front of her.

She was deep in concentration. I'm not even sure she saw me, but I'm sure she did.

The chickadees were flying about, waiting for Graham to finish filling the feeders.

I watched in horror as one of the little silver chickadees flew right into the window near Bailey. It didn't fall to the ground though. Instead the wind must have caught it, keeping it from hitting the ground right away, and swept it away.

Spinning drunkenly in the wind, it crashed a second time into the side of the gazebo.

I gathered up my skirts and ran as quickly as one could run through the deepening snow to reach the bird.

It was doubtless a foolhardy thing to do, but I was acting on instinct.

As I neared the gazebo, I couldn't see it. It must have gotten buried in the snow when it crashed.

It would freeze to death in no time.

"Dakota," Zachary called out. "What are you doing?"

I was almost there. Almost to the place I had seen it crash into the gazebo.

I looked back over my shoulder. "A bird," I said.

But just as I turned back, my feet got tangled in my skirts and I knew I was going down. I was going down and there was nothing I could do about it.

I crashed headlong into the gazebo.

As I fell, I saw the bird, not moving. I'd found him.

But I had fallen, too.

I couldn't help him.

"Dakota!" I heard Zachary's voice over the wind, over the ringing in my ears.

But then I heard nothing.

CHAPTER 34
ZACHARY

*J*ust as I turned, I saw Dakota falling. At first I thought she was diving into the snow on purpose, but she wouldn't do that.

And why had she been rushing down the hill, gentle as it was, toward the gazebo?

I dropped the bucket of birdseed and took off after her.

She wasn't moving.

No. Oh no.

Not this.

Not Dakota.

I had not come all this way to fall in love only to lose her.

She was perfect. We were perfect.

"Dakota," I reached her side and gathered her into my arms.

Her eyes were closed. I drew her against me.

That's when I saw the little chickadee lying in the snow. When it blinked, I understood what Dakota had been doing. She had been coming to rescue this bird.

I'd heard her say the word *bird*.

"Is she okay?" Graham asked, coming up behind me.

"I don't know," I said. "She's unconscious."

"I know first aid," Graham said, opening the gazebo door. "Bring her in here."

I picked her up and carried her through the gazebo door. Laid her gently on the cold floor.

"Do you have a blanket?" I asked.

"Not in here," Graham said, checking Dakota's pulse. "Pulse is good. She's breathing. Try to keep her warm."

I gathered her to me. "What's wrong with her?" I asked.

"I don't know. Maybe she hit her head."

"Maybe," I said, fighting against the lump in my throat.

"We need to get her into the house. Get her warm. Can you carry her?"

"Of course." She weighed hardly anything, but the layers and layers she was wearing was another story.

"Why is she out?" I asked, hearing the panic in my own voice.

"The cold. The elevation. The shock of falling down. But probably hit head head."

"The bird," I said. "Get the bird."

"What bird?" Graham asked.

"The bird just outside the door in the snow."

I hugged Dakota against me, willing her to wake up.

Graham came back with a small chickadee in his gloved hands. "Is this what she was after?" he asked.

"I think so."

"Well," Graham said. "It's knocked out, too."

"Let's get them both inside the house," I said. "Get them warmed up."

The French doors to the gazebo banged closed with a gust of wind.

With the little bird in one hand, Graham pushed open the door. "I'll hold the door," he said, stepping outside.

I got on my knees and gathered Dakota in my arms.

"Wake up," I said. "Dakota. Wake up."

Then I was sitting on the floor of the gazebo.

Alone.

Absolutely alone.

CHAPTER 35
DAKOTA

I woke disoriented.

It took me a minute, but I realized I was in my own bed.

And I was warm.

The last bit of evening sun lit the room along with a blazing fire and several candles.

I turned my head and saw Bailey sitting in a chair next to the bed.

"Dakota," she said, seeing me awake.

"What? What are you doing here?"

"You…" She stopped, trying to decide how to tell me. I sat up, leaving me feeling a little dizzy.

"Don't try to get up," she said. "You fell down. Bumped your head."

I laid back down and tried to remember. Yes. I had fallen down. The bird.

"There was a chickadee," I said. "It hit the window."

"Yes." Bailey smiled, just a little.

"Is it okay?"

"It's somewhere in the house. Flying around."

"In the house?" I asked. "How did that happen? He flew into the window."

"Graham… actually Benson… brought him inside and he quickly came to."

"So he's okay?"

"He's fine."

I closed my eyes. I fell down. Bumped my head.

"Zachary," I said, turning and looking at Bailey again.

"Dakota," she said. "When you fell down, you were near the gazebo. Zachary and Graham took you into the gazebo to get you out of the wind."

I was shaking my head.

"Where is he?" I asked. "Where is Zachary?"

Bailey lifted her chin. Took a deep breath.

"He went back through time."

"No," I said. "How do you know?"

"I know because he was there. And then he wasn't."

"But why?" I felt the panic rising in my throat. Zachary was gone.

"The gazebo," she said. "It's his portal."

Of course it was. It made sense somehow. But…

"Where's the book?" I asked. "Where's the *Lavender Blue* book?"

Bailey went to my dresser. Picked up the book and brought it back to me.

"I spent some time reading it," she said. "It's a bit humbling."

I knew what she meant, but I didn't have time to talk to her about that right now.

I flipped to the back. To the photographs. I slowly turned the page.

The photograph of me and Zachary was still there.

"It's still here," I said. "He's here. That means he'll be back."

Bailey shook her head. "Graham and I think…" She put a hand on mine. "We think it's still there because this book came from the future. If you went to the future and bought this same book, he wouldn't be in it."

"No," I said. "You don't know that. You can't know."

"It's what makes sense," she said. "But, no, I can't know."

"How do we get him back?" I asked. "How?"

"Dakota," Bailey said. "We don't get him back. He has to come back on his on."

"What if he doesn't? What if he can't?" I'd only felt this helpless one other time. When our mother had been sick.

But even with that, this was different.

Not worse, just different.

I had imagined a life with Zachary. He had asked me to marry him. We were going to get married.

"No," I said, relaxing my head back on the pillow.

"You should rest," Bailey said. "Graham thinks you passed out from the cold and the exertion. Bumped her head. But you should rest. I'll have Anna bring you some hot soup."

I didn't answer. I couldn't.

I heard her footsteps cross the room. Heard the door close behind her.

I just lay there with my eyes closed. The tears spilling out of my eyes as my broken heart shattered into a million pieces.

CHAPTER 36
DAKOTA

Three weeks Later

I sat at the grand piano, lightly touching the keys. Not
playing anything. Just tapping random keys. Letting
the sound echo through the house, then touching another
single key.

I rested my elbow on the space behind the keys and my
head on my left hand.

It had been three weeks since I had fallen down in the snow
outside the gazebo.

Three weeks since Zachary had tried to save me by taking
me into the very place that sent him back to the future.

Had he thought about that? Or had he just done it without
thinking?

Would I ever know?

I kept the *Lavender Blue* book on my nightstand and I spent
hours staring at his photograph.

I didn't understand how it could be this way.

How he had been here. And then gone so quickly.

How there was a photograph of the two of us together when we had not taken that photograph.

Bailey and Graham didn't know if he would be back.

I didn't know how he couldn't come back.

According to the time travel spell in his blood, he had to come back.

Bailey had waited for Graham when he had gone back through time. Until she didn't. She had become engaged to someone else. The whole thing had almost ended in disaster after Graham had come back after all.

But I wasn't going to do that.

I was never going to give up on Zachary.

I could live here with Bailey or I could go back to Whiskey Springs and live in our house there. If I had to, I would get a place of my own.

But I wanted to stay here. Right here. Near the gazebo.

The gazebo was Zachary's portal. If... when... he came back, he would come back through the gazebo. Even if Bailey and Graham kicked me out, they could tell Zachary where to find me.

I hit another key. This one deep and mournful.

By day, I walked around the house in a daze. The snow was too heavy for me to go outside. When I wasn't wandering the house, I stood at my window and watched the gazebo, willing Zachary to come back.

But all the willing in the world did not appear to be bringing him back.

At night, I slept fitfully. Tossing and turning. Bad dreams. So I'd get up and wander the house some more.

"Miss Dakota," Anna called.

I looked up at Anna. Anna, like everyone else had done everything they could to pull me out of my despondency.

"Come quick," she said. "It's Mistress Bailey. The baby is coming."

I sat up straight. "Now?"

"Yes ma'am."

"But it's too early. Isn't it?"

"A baby comes when its ready," she said.

I left the piano and followed Anna up to Bailey's bedroom.

Graham was there holding her hand.

"Do you know what to do, Anna?" I asked.

"Yes ma'am," Anna said. "I know. But you have to help me."

"Me?" I stood frozen in the middle of the room, shaking my head. "I don't know anything about babies, much less birthing."

"Well, you're about to learn," Anna said. "There's no one else."

There's no one else.

Anna was right.

There was no one else.

It didn't even occur to me to question why Graham was in the room during the birth. Graham did everything with Bailey. Why should this be any different?

CHAPTER 37
DAKOTA

$\mathcal{I}$ stood at the window in the little nursery on the second floor.

Rocking little Annabella, all swaddled in a blanket, in my arms.

I could see the gazebo from here just as I could from my bedroom. Maybe it was an even better view.

A few snowflakes fell softly, but the worst of the storm had moved out.

It would be Christmastime soon. A time when the house world normally be decked in silver and gold. A Christmas tree. But everything was different this year.

The baby cooed and I looked down into her sweet face. She looked like Bailey. So much like her. But I could see Graham's eyes in her.

It was amazing how the two of them had magically created a little being that was a mixture of both of them.

Two beautiful people had come together to make a beautiful little person.

I stood there, watching the sunset over the mountains.

And I longed for something I could not have.

My own little family. With Zachary.

I understood now how Bailey had decided to marry someone else when Graham had not returned. I understood that need, reluctant as it may be, to go on with one's life.

I didn't like it, but I understood it.

With the sun behind the mountains, I left the window.

Maybe I did need to leave here. It was impossible not to watch for Zachary. Hoping he would magically return.

It was time for Annabella to eat. I kissed her on the forehead and took her back into Bailey's room.

"How are you feeling?" I asked.

Bailey sat up and took Annabella into her arms, her whole face lighting up.

"Better," she said.

The birth had been hard on Bailey.

She'd done it all without a doctor.

I now had a whole new level of respect for Anna. I no longer thought of her as a lady in waiting. Anna was an amazing woman.

"Sit," Bailey said, patting the side of her bed while she took care of feeding Annabella.

I sat next to her.

"I've been there," she said. "I know it's different for everybody, but I have an idea of what you're going through."

"I know," I said. "I was there, remember?"

She smiled. "I remember. I confess, I didn't know what to do. But it was a little different for me."

"How so?"

"Graham and I hadn't been as close as you and Zachary."

"We were going to get married." The words came out as a whisper.

"I know," she said, putting a hand over mine. You always have a place here. You know that, right?"

"I know. Thank you."

"Now," Bailey said. "We need to talk about decorating this house for Christmas."

"Nobody's going to see it but us," I said.

"Dakota Auclair," she said. "Aren't we just as important as anyone else?"

"Of course we are," I said.

"That's right. Give me a couple more days and we're going to start decking these halls with everything Christmas. We deserve to enjoy it as much if not more than anyone else."

Bailey was right. We were all important.

We could decorate the house just for us to enjoy.

Bailey, Graham, Benson, Anna, and me. Even little Annabella.

We were family.

Graham was good for her. Very good for her.

And it was time for me to pull myself up by the bootstraps and get on with my life.

I didn't have to marry anyone, but I had things I needed to be doing.

My life was important, too.

CHAPTER 38
DAKOTA

"Graham hates it when we get on a ladder," Bailey said as I stepped onto the ladder to place a wax coated pinecone on the tree.

"I know," I said. "But he isn't here, is he?"

"Not at the moment. But if you fall off, I suppose he'll find out."

Graham had gone out hunting. Annabella slept in her crib. The baby actually had three cribs. One downstairs in the parlor. One in the nursery—actually in Bailey and Graham's bedroom at the moment, and one on the fourth floor next to Bailey's work area.

"Hand me another one," I said.

Bailey handed me another pinecone. We had spent all afternoon yesterday dipping pinecones, some in red wax, some in silver, some in both. Where they got red and silver coloring for the wax was beyond me, but somehow Graham could come up with things no one else could.

In some of my more fanciful moments, I imagined that when he went out hunting, he was actually going to the future to bring things back here.

But then he'd show up with a deer or something that would keep us fed and I would come back to reality. He was simply out hunting.

"Mistress Bailey," Benson said, standing at the doorway. "Mister Graham is back. He asked me to let you know."

Bailey's face lit up as it always did when Graham returned from anywhere.

"Will you watch Annabella?" she asked.

"Of course."

"And get off that ladder."

"Of course," I said again, but while I was here, I decided to do some rearranging. The pinecones were too close together. I needed to add some more silver ones on this side. Move the red ones...

"How about a red one right there?"

I lifted the red pinecone, then just held it. Frozen in place.

I knew that voice. But no.

I was imagining things again.

Holding the pinecone, I forced my brain to function. Tried anyway.

Still holding the red pinecone, I looked over my shoulder.

And when I did, I started falling backwards through the air.

But I quickly realized I wasn't falling. At least not exactly.

I grabbed hold of the first thing I could and that just happened to be Zachary.

Zachary.

"Hi," he said, smiling into my eyes.

I couldn't speak. I truly just could not get words to form in my head much less say them out loud.

My heart was pounding nearly out of my chest.

When he turned around in a circle, me hanging on for dear life, I laughed.

"Zachary," I said, placing a hand on his cheek.

"How are you, Love?" he asked.

I blinked rapidly. I would not cry.

Would not.

But he kissed away the tears anyway.

"It's really you," I said, barely able to speak.

"It's really me."

I took a deep ragged breath. "What took you so long?"

"I had some things to take care of," he said.

I scowled at him and found my voice. "That's all? Just some things?"

"Important things." He moved to kiss me, then stopped. "Please tell me you didn't marry someone else while I was gone."

I grinned. "No. I did not marry anyone else."

"And that baby." He nodded toward Annabella. "That's Bailey's? Right?"

"You are incorrigible."

"And you are beautiful."

Something fluttered in the tree, capturing Zachary's attention.

"I think there's something in the tree," he said.

"That's Champagne," I said.

"Who's Champagne?"

"The bird."

"You have a bird loose in your house?"

Champagne chose that moment to fly out of the tree, make a circle around the parlor, then went to sit on a limb, looking at us.

"Champagne," I said. "Remember the bird that ran into the window?"

"How could I forget?" he said. "Please tell me you don't have a bird flying loose in the house. With a baby."

"Of course not. Benson has a cage for him, but he really likes the tree. It seemed like giving him a home was the least we could do."

Zachary just looked at me like I had lost my mind.

"Don't worry. He's just visiting," I said. "Do you really think Graham would let a wild bird near his baby without supervision?"

"No." He let me slide to the floor. "Of course not."

I grinned, enjoying torturing him, just a little.

"I'm glad we got that settled," he said, looking warily toward Champagne.

"Me too."

"Where were we?" he asked.

"I think you were telling me why you were gone so long."

"Nope," he said. "Wasn't that." He gathered me in his arms. Cupped my chin in his hand and pressed his lips to mine.

I sank against him.

This. This put everything back right again.

This was just as things were supposed to be.

"You knew I was coming back, right?" he asked, his lips close to mine.

"I never had a single doubt," I said.

He grinned and kissed me again.

Champagne started singing.

Then Annabella started to cry.

"Things are not as I left them," he said.

"Maybe." I grinned. "But the important things are."

My heart was most definitely where he had left it. In his hands.

EPILOGUE

We sat in the parlor, the tall Christmas tree, decorated in red and silver, in front of us.

Pinecones. Ribbons and bows. Glass balls Graham had ordered from somewhere. Probably special made.

The fire crackled in the fireplace, providing not only warmth and light, but also a warm, cozy ambiance.

Graham and Bailey sat together with Annabella in Graham's lap. He had bought her all sorts of toys she was too young for. A wooden wagon. A little rocking chair. Dolls.

But she just cooed and smiled at her doting parents.

I sat on the other sofa next to Zachary.

He pulled me close and kissed my cheek.

"I have something for you," he said.

"You're here," I said. "That's all that matters."

"Actually," he said. "I have two things for you."

"Okay," I said. "What?"

"Wait," he said. "Be patient."

I put my hands in my lap. Pretended to look patient.

He laughed.

"Okay. One of them you get to keep. The other one you can't keep, at least not for very long."

"Why can't I keep it?" Why would he give me something I couldn't keep?

"Because if you keep it, it has no value. It's like a gift card."

I shook my head. "You're speaking future talk again."

"Which one do you want first?" he asked.

"The one I can keep, I guess."

He reached into his pocket and pulled a little square robin's egg blue box tied with a white ribbon. "Have you ever heard of Tiffany's?" he asked.

"I don't know. Maybe." Bailey had a lot of fashion magazines. Sometimes I looked at them.

"Well, this is from Tiffany's." He leaned closed and whispered. "Future Tiffany's."

"It's so pretty. Can I open it?"

"Of course," he said.

I untied the ribbon and opened the box. It contained another box, a velvet one.

"Can I borrow it?" he asked before I opened it.

"I thought you said I could keep this one."

He laughed. "You can have it right back."

Then he was down on one knee.

"Remember that preliminary proposal I made out on the mountainside?"

"Of course."

"This one is official." He opened the box, revealing a sparkling solitaire diamond ring on a silver band.

He slid it onto my ring finger.

"It's beautiful," I said, my eyes misting over.

"Happy tears?" he asked, kissing them away.

I nodded.

"Dakota Auclair," he said. "Will you marry me and spend the rest of time with me?"

"Yes," I said, falling into his arms.

Annabella started crying.

"Congratulations," Bailey and Graham said, juggling their baby.

"I have one more for you," Zachary said.

"The one I can't keep?"

"That's right."

"We'll be right back," Bailey said. "This little one needs some attention."

"We'll ask Benson to send in hot chocolate," Graham said.

After they were gone, Zachary handed me another box. This one flat and square and wrapped with red paper and a silver bow.

It was a bracelet with about a dozen gold charms and half a dozen silver ones.

"It's beautiful," I said, then looked at Zachary in confusion. "Why can't I keep it?"

"Because anytime you need money, you go into the bank and take one of these little charms off. It'll buy you anything you want."

"You gave me… money?"

"Consider it a wedding present," he said. "As long as you have this, you'll have anything you need."

"I didn't get you anything," I said.

"You did. You've given my life meaning. You've given me true love."

I grinned up at him. "Then the love spell running through your blood worked?"

"I guess it did."

I guess it did.

Zachary pulled me into his lap and kissed me.

"Promise me something," I said against his lips.

"Anything."

"Promise me you'll never go into the gazebo again."

"I've already talked to Graham about tearing it down."

"What if you change your mind?"

"I can promise that I will never, ever change my mind."

"It was built just for us then. To bring us together."

"So it seems," he said, kissing me again.

We'd found each other and we were never letting go.

The little bird, Champagne flew out of tree, circling around us before going back to the nest we had made for him. One day, in the spring maybe he would go, but for now he had a home here with us.

With a light snowfall outside, we were safe and warm inside. I held out my hand, admiring the diamond ring as the firelight reflected off of it.

Needing a husband, it seemed, was a far different thing from wanting one.

Either way I had found the one for me.

Keep Reading for a preview of Twilight Frost...

TWILIGHT FROST PREVIEW

Prologue

*E*very Christmas Eve at twilight a ghost appeared in front of the old Colorado blue spruce in Auclair Memorial Park.

Not just any ghost, but the ghost of Elise Auclair.

No one ever questioned that it was Elise.

According to the legend of Whiskey Springs, Elise waited there for her one true love.

They made a promise to meet there, but he never returned.

So she came back every year. Year after year.

Waiting…

Chapter 1
Benjamin Smith

TODAY

. . .

"You have got to be—" I bit my tongue. "A week?"

In my eight years as a pilot, I had never once had a flat tire on an airplane.

Until today.

After grabbing a quick hamburger at the edge of town, I'd come back to the airport, a generous term for what was little more than a runway, just outside the small mountain town of Whiskey Springs to run through my preflight checklist and do a walk around.

A flat tire.

Normally a flat tire would be no problem. But here at this airport they had no way to fix a flat. No replacement tires or even the right kind of valve for me to fix it myself.

So I had to wait. A winter snow storm was keeping any kind of courier from getting through. It didn't help that the holidays were here.

I called everywhere and everyone I knew who might have any kind of solution.

Opening my iPad, I checked the weather. Snow. And not just snow. Heavy snow.

A winter storm warning.

This storm had not been in the forecast.

Maybe on one of the obscure ones that I checked on occasion, but not the National Weather Service. Not on NOAA.

A freak snow storm, they were calling it.

And I just happened to be sitting here with a flat tire.

Less than one week until Christmas. My sister's wedding in Houston. On Christmas Eve.

I gave some serious thought to flying anyway. Knelt down on the tarmac and ran my hand along the nitrogen tire. I was certain it was the valve stem, but there was a puncture hole near it, too.

Standing up, I looked toward the mountain peaks, snow clouds clustered around them. Definitely snow in the high country.

The wind, much stronger than it had been when I had landed, whipped at my coat. Definitely stronger than it had been just over an hour ago. I pulled off my hat and tossed it inside the cockpit then climbed inside.

My mentor, Noah Worthington, had drilled safety into my head above all else. *A reckless pilot is a dead pilot* he would say.

I made the phone calls I needed to make. Ordered what I needed to order. When the weather cleared my tire would be on the way. Then I got to work busy finding myself a place to stay.

All the major hotels were booked. The weather, of course. And on top of that it was a week before Christmas.

Everyone recommended the Auclair House, a bed and breakfast on the north side of town.

Unable to find anything online about it, I called the number the guy at the Holiday Inn gave me.

The young lady who answered the phone claimed to have one room left. I made a reservation with my credit card, called an Uber, and headed in that direction.

The Uber driver was chatty. Although I wasn't in the mood, I heard every word he said.

"That's the Whiskey Springs Saloon," he said. "Started the whole town right there. It was a boarding house, an entertainment house, and a saloon all at the same time."

It looked rather small to have served all those purposes, but it had a fresh coat of paint and some plate glass windows that obviously had been added later. It had obviously been taken care of over the years.

It was dead center in the middle of town, so it looked like the town had spread out around it, like he said.

"On the left over there is the park. It's only been a park for about a hundred years or so give or take a few decades. It started off as one of Bailey Auclair's favorite places to come and paint."

"Who's that?" I asked when he took a breath.

"Famous artist. You're not from here," he said, not even pausing for confirmation. "That Colorado blue spruce has been there for probably eight hundred years."

"Looks like it," I said under my breath, but he heard me and sent me a look.

"It's a short walk from the park—The Auclair Memorial Park—to the Auclair Bed and Breakfast where you'll be staying. You should walk down there. Most folks appreciate it."

"The Auclairs are a big name around here."

"They weren't the first ones here, but they made their place here in town, as well as having property on the other side of the park."

"Impressive," I said, a little curious in spite of myself about this Auclair family.

"You'll see their name alongside Dr. Alexander Avery's. He was a major founder of the town."

"What did the Auclairs do?" I asked.

"Only two of them ended up staying in town," he said. "For different reasons. The girl stayed the longest."

He stopped the car at the curb in front of a rather large two-story house that was definitely old. I preferred the modern conveniences of hotels over the older bed and breakfasts. Room service. Televisions. Plenty of hot water.

"We're here," the driver said. "Told you it wasn't far from the park."

I only had a small overnight bag with me. The one I always kept in the plane with me. Just in case. Didn't have any winter clothes in there though, so I was going to be making a shopping trip downtown tonight or in the morning.

Fortunately it was a short walk to town so I could easily avoid having to call a driver.

"Doesn't look like much on the outside," the driver said. "But it's nice on the inside. Been kept up to date." Seems the Uber driver was a mind reader, too.

Now that I was here I started thinking just how nice it was going to be to have a few days to myself. I had a lot of alone time to think in the cockpit, but being able to walk around, look at different things, that was long overdue.

There was only one definite downside. I had to call my sister. Let her know I wasn't going to make it to her wedding.

I'd never tell her, but there were worse things than missing a wedding with two thousand guests. Maybe not two thousand, but might as well be. I seriously doubted she'd even miss me other than maybe at picture taking time.

The Uber driver had told me the truth. The inside of the house was elegantly furnished. Decked out in Christmas colors of crimson and silver. A huge fir tree took up one quadrant of the living room that served as a lobby, festively lit with thousands of clear twinkling lights. Red and silver wax coated pine cones. And glass balls of all sorts.

I wondered what was up with the wax coated pine cones.

"Mr. Smith," the girl I had talked to behind the counter greeted me.

I nodded.

"Welcome to the Auclair Bed and Breakfast." She smiled. She was most definitely not from here. She had a southern accent that I could spot a mile away. I had an aunt from Alabama and I would put money on her being from there. Birmingham maybe. Or Auburn.

"Do you have more luggage?" she asked.

"It was an unplanned trip," I said.

"Right. You're the pilot," she said.

"That's right," I said. "Word travels fast."

"Small town," she said, with a little shrug. "Your room is on the second floor just up the stairs and to the right. You'll have a great view of downtown from there. And if you listen on a clear night, you can hear music coming from the saloon."

"Do I need to fill anything out?"

"Nah. It's a bed and breakfast. Not a big chain hotel." She smiled. "Besides, your credit card went through so you're good."

She slid a key across the counter. "Breakfast at six. Or you can have something sent up later."

"I'll just have something sent up." After I got off the phone with my family, I was going to need some sleep.

"Just call down when you're ready for breakfast," she said. "Have a good night."

It was only four o'clock in the afternoon. As I went up the stairs decked out with flocked green garland wrapped around the bannister, the grandfather clock began to chime the hour.

Four chimes, the last one hanging in the air as I reached the second floor.

It felt like a whole lot later though, especially with the early evening darkness settling in.

I went inside my room, sprawled across the bed and kicked off my shoes.

Maybe I'd just take a nap before making my phone calls.

After about half a minute, my phone started vibrating.

With a groan, I sat up and loosened my tie.

There was a letter on my nightstand, my name scrawled across the front in a girlish handwriting.

Nice touch, I thought.

I picked up the letter. It was sealed, so I checked my phone messages first.

NICOLE: *Saw the storm on the Weather Channel. Please tell me you're on your way back to Houston.*

Might as well get the worst of it over with. Rip off the band-aid.

ME: *Bad news. Had a flat tire in Whiskey Springs. But I'm ok.*

I added that last part in there just to temper her reaction. Normally Nicole thought of others before herself, but with her wedding being in merely days, I knew that was not going to be the case.

Thought bubbles.

Since I really didn't want to know what she had to say right now, I set my phone on the nightstand, face down. It wasn't like I could do anything about it. Stranded was stranded. My family knew it was a hazard of being a private airplane pilot.

I laid back on the bed and unfolded the letter addressed to me.

Dear Benjamin,
I know you had to go. That you had no choice.
I'll just say it. Please come back.
If you believe... If you believe in us...
Meet me at the park at Twilight tonight. Christmas Eve.
I'll be there. Waiting for you.
No matter when. I'll be there.
Please don't leave me here without you.
Yours forever,
Elise

Feeling like I had intruded on someone else's personal correspondence, I quickly refolded the letter and put it back on the nightstand.

Smith was a common last name. Benjamin Smith not so much.

But this was obviously a mistake.

I would take it downstairs later. Give it to the girl behind the desk.

Let her find out who it really belonged to.

Chapter 2
Elise Auclair

1869
Whiskey Springs

I HUMMED to myself as I arranged decorations in the display window.

My shop had the only display window in Whiskey Springs and I was rather proud of that fact.

My little store had only one window, to the left as you walk in the front door, so I needed lots of candles to keep things bright.

It didn't matter that my display window was little more than a window seat with a wide shelf, it was still a store front window and I treated it as such.

I decorated it with two oversized handwoven reed baskets with rope handles. One overflowing with red wax coated pinecones and the other overflowing with silver wax coated pinecones.

After backing up and studying it for a moment, I tipped the baskets over, arranging the pinecones to look like they were spilling out.

I added a couple of books and rounded it off with a frilly straw hat I'd ordered from a dressmaker in Boston.

As for the pinecones, my sister, Bailey, had started the whole thing last Christmas during a terrible blizzard.

Her husband, an innovative man had given her the idea and Bailey had run with it.

The best part was that my little shop was the only place around here to buy the wax-coated pinecones.

Personally, I liked the two colors, red and silver, together for Christmas enough to adopt them for my own decoration theme in my own house.

The Christmas tree in one corner of my shop was festively decorated with some of those silver and red pinecones. Silver and red ribbons and bows cascading over it. And glass balls that had come from back east. Everything on the tree was for sale.

Someday we wouldn't have to order things from back east. Someday Whiskey Springs would be big enough that we would have everything we needed right here. That was, at least, my hope.

I went back behind the counter and straightened a glass jar filled with little peppermint sticks. Took one out and popped it in my mouth.

Everything looked ready for business, so I unlocked the front doors. Less than one week before Christmas. A good time for my grand opening.

Today was opening day. I was a little bit nervous, wondering how many customers I would have. Several townspeople had stopped by while I was getting everything ready and they had all been encouraging. All of them agreed that Whiskey Springs needed a shop like this.

I sat behind the counter and watched the morning traffic outside the front of my shop. People walking here and there. Horses and buggies passing by. A stagecoach rumbled past, leaving town.

After about an hour of not having any customers, I went into the back room for a drink of water.

The shop had been merely something I wanted to do. Not something I had to do.

I'd enjoyed the planning, the shopping, the setting up.

Now it was mine.

The downside of that was that I had sunk most everything I had into it. So now I was committed.

Still, if not a single customer walked through that door, I had done what I wanted to do. And yet it had taken on an importance of its own.

As the youngest of five siblings, that had not been easy. All of my sisters and even my brother had their own ideas about how I should live my life.

Get married and have a family. That was, of course, the most popular suggestion, but it was expected of all young ladies. I wasn't going to just willy-nilly pick some man and marry him for the sake of getting married. I had my own thoughts on that one.

Start a school and teach. Whiskey Springs had no school and, granted, it would have satisfied my entrepreneurial spirit, but teaching was not my passion. Neither were children. I didn't dislike children, I just didn't necessarily like them.

Work as a seamstress and do sewing for people. Sitting alone all day sewing for people might have meaningful for any of my other sisters, but not me. I liked people. I liked having people around to talk to. That was one of the reasons I had opened this store. My three older sisters had married and moved out, leaving just me and my brother. My brother, Colton, had a wandering spirit so he was rarely home. That left me there alone.

Long ago, back when we lived in Mississippi, I'd seen a painting of a department store in London that had a lovely front display window. That image had stayed with me and I'd often imagined what it would be like to have own shop window to decorate.

The little bell tinkled alerting me that someone had walked into my store.

Delighted, I hurried back out to stand behind the counter.

A handsome man stood there, just inside the door, looking around.

All in black, he was wearing a long wool coat, leather gloves, and a warm cap. He held a red shopping bag in one hand.

"Hello," I said, with a smile. "Welcome."

"Hi," he said, looking at me with a rather perplexed expression.

"What are you looking for?"

"I'm not sure," he said, his gaze flicking over in the direction of the Christmas tree.

"Is it for a Christmas gift?"

He turned and looked into my eyes.

"A wedding gift," he said. "For my sister."

I grinned. "She's getting married? That's wonderful. When?"

"Christmas Eve," he said.

"That's exciting," I said. "What a wonderful day to get married. It's my favorite day in the whole year."

He just looked at me.

"Do you want help or do you just want to look around?" I asked.

I honestly had not expected my first customer to be a man. I didn't know much about how men shopped, except for my brother Colton. And I'd only seen him buy things like flour at the General Store.

"I don't know yet," he said. "I guess I'll look around some."

"Okay." I smiled and sat down on my stool. I rested my elbows on the counter and my chin on my hands to watch him.

He walked over to the tree and lightly touched one of the red ribbons.

"You're my first customer," I said, standing up and smiling broadly.

Chapter 3
Benjamin

I'D DECIDED that it would be best to go into town today since it looked like the storm would be coming in hard tonight.

I needed to get some heavy boots to wear in the snow if nothing else.

A week. It was still sinking in that I was going to have to spend a whole week here in Whiskey Springs. It wasn't that it was a bad little town. It was actually quaint and historical with a certain charm.

It was just... this was Christmas week. I would be missing all the Christmas gatherings. The office party.

My sister's wedding.

I did not mind missing the wedding. But the wrath of both my sister and my mother would come down on my head.

It wasn't even that I was all that close to my family. We all just sort of did our own thing.

"Are you new here then?" I asked. If I was her first customer, she must be new.

The girl behind the counter was young and obviously quite naïve.

"New?" she asked. "The store just opened today."

A quick gaze around told me everything did look new. Old-fashioned, but new.

"I see," I said.

It was a rather eclectic shop. Obviously designed for women. Christmas decorations—lots of those. Candles. Books.

The young lady came out from behind the counter and I blinked hard.

She was wearing a long dress. Not just long, but old-fashioned.

Old-fashioned was definitely the theme in here.

The skirts of her silver dress belled out around her. The dress had a high neckline and long sleeves. Her dark brunette hair fell loosely around her shoulders.

She had a classic heart-shaded face with smooth delicate skin and pink bow-shaped lips.

She looked just like a southern belle. It was a rather charming outfit and she wore it well.

"I have lots of Christmas decorations," she said. "But that probably wouldn't make a good wedding gift." She tapped a finger against her chin, deep in thought.

"A candle, maybe?" she suggested.

"Maybe." I was intrigued by her and had quite honestly lost interest in buying a gift for my sister, since I hadn't had a whole lot to begin with. I'd already spent a fortune buying a silverware set off her wedding registry at Williams Sonoma.

I had only ducked in here to get warm before heading back to the bed and breakfast.

"Why don't you give me a tour?" I asked.

Her face brightened. "Okay."

Deftly managing the skirts of her dress, she walked first to the Christmas tree. "All of these decorations are for sale, of course. The pinecones are all hand-dipped in red and silver wax."

"Who dipped them?" I asked.

"I did," she said, then kept going without a hitch. "There are lots of different kinds of decorations on here."

She carefully plucked one from the tree. "This is my favorite one," she said, holding it out in her palm for me to see.

I leaned close to look at it. The sparkly glass ornament had a tiny little cottage inside it. Sort of like a ship in a bottle, except it was a cottage in a ball. Sort of like a snow globe without the snow.

"This is beautiful," I said. "You made this, too?"

"No, Silly," she said, with a little laugh. "These are imported from a glass-blower on the east coast."

"It's the prettiest ornament I've ever seen." I looked at her. And she was one of the prettiest girls. She had an innocence about her and a friendly charm that could not be feigned.

"It really is," she said, looking at it again.

"I'd like to buy it," I said.

"Okay." Her smile faltered just a little. She seemed pulled between making a sale and selling her favorite ornament.

"Is this the only one like it that you have?" I asked.

"They're all hand-made one of a kind."

"You should keep it," I said.

"No, of course not," she said, smiling again. "It's for purchase. I'll wrap it up for you."

In the spirit of Christmas, I knew what I was going to do with it. I was going to give it to her.

She carefully wrapped the ornament in a velvet cloth and placed it in my hands.

"Put this in your pocket," she said.

"But I haven't paid for it."

"I'll start a tab for you," she said. "You can settle up in a bit."

"Okay," I said. "But you have to let me pay you before I leave."

"Okay. "She put her hands behind her back. "Anything else?" she asked,

"I don't know," I said. "What about the rest of my tour?"

"Oh. Of course."

I noticed there were paintings scattered on all the walls.

She walked towards a wall of shelves. It held a few books. Frilly hats. A little tea set.

"What's the name of your store again?" I asked, noticing a classic teddy bear on one of the shelves.

She stopped and turned to look at me. "I don't know. I haven't named it yet."

"You haven't—" I watched her closely. She seemed serious.

I'd seen the name over the door. It was something... Gifts or...

"Timeless Keepsakes," I said.

"That's so perfect," she said. "I love it. Timeless Keepsakes it is."

An older woman came into the store. "I need to... um." She gestured toward the woman.

"Go," I said. "I'll wait here."

I wasn't going anywhere. The older woman who just came inside was also wearing a long dress, though it wasn't nearly as fetching on her as it was..."

Hell. I didn't even know the young lady's name.

I was going to stay right here until I figured some things out.

Keep Reading Twilight Frost...

Kathryn Kaleigh is the author of over seventy novels, over one hundred short stories, and many collections.

kathrynkaleigh.com

www.ingramcontent.com/pod-product-compliance
Lightning Source LLC
Chambersburg PA
CBHW050450110726
47899CB00003B/889